SOUTH

SOUTH

ASPECTS AND IMAGES

FROM CORSICA, ITALY,

AND SOUTHERN FRANCE

WILLIAM SANSOM

HARCOURT, BRACE AND COMPANY, NEW YORK

The characters in this book are entirely
imaginary and bear no relation to any living person.

CONTENTS

SOUTH

For N. O.
in gratitude

MY LITTLE ROBINS

THAT notable engineer first made his appearance one night on the Ligurian Sea, on the Ajaccio passage.

At nine or ten o'clock I was sitting huddled in a corner of the second-class saloon. One heavily shaded light burned above a flap-table that served, with its four or five bottles, as a bar. The rest of the saloon faded off on all sides into darkness, the darkness of bulwark-shaped walls and a portholed fore-partition: in the darkness lay passengers in all the humped and sprawled positions of shipboard sleep. They lay among the litter of their suppers—bread-rind, cheese-crumbs, wine bottles—and the crumpled shreds of newspaper in which all that food had been wrapped; among the first pale reachings of vomit; against shoulders and on laps, on Corsicans sailing back to their native island, on Corsican nieces visiting their old aunts in mountain villages, on Corsican entrepreneurs of Ajaccio, on the sons of Corsicans returning from their universities in France, on Corsican travellers in chestnuts and granite and wood, on long-moustached migrants homing again, on matriarchs intent upon the hearths of their first brood-ing—on all these who were bound together by the second-class look, dark and roughish, bound with the wicker-basket and the peasant spattering that distinguish both ships bound for islands and ships of the inland seas, rough ships that ply the Black Sea, the Caspian, the local Baltic and this the Ligurian Sea bound for Ajaccio in French Corsica.

And now into this sleep-smelling saloon, shuddering from the engines aft, dusky with the cramp of travellers,

7

there stepped the bright-blue dungarees of an engineer.
He entered firmly, straight from his engines, with a
seaman's tread; stood for a moment wiping some of the
oil from his hands; stepped over to the circle of light over
the makeshift bar. Disregarding the passengers, he fingered a packet of cigarettes from his dungaree pockets,
held it high to drop a cigarette unsoiled into his mouth,
then ordered a pastis. He held the milky glass outstretched, curling out one long finger in a gesture of stiff
delicacy—and drank. This man's presence was forceful—
instantly one was affected. There was nothing odd in what
he did—though later it was to prove otherwise. The
appearance in the second-class saloon of a ship's worker,
an ordinary engineer, was not unusual to any but a few
northern passengers accustomed to firmer disciplinary
divisions on larger and colder ships. It was more his personal figure; and, of course, some essential power beneath
this.

He did not look like what an engineer might be supposed to look. He was a tall, thin, gangling man, with a
beaked nose and dark bright eyes that peered forward
with the look of an angry scholar. His thin stomach
arched in, his knees knobbled and bent forward, his arms
held bonily akimbo, he moved—and he moved all the
time, he never stopped—like an agitated don doing his
best with a fox-trot. Often the scholarly, the nominally
unworldly, lurch and stumble not so much because their
bodies have been misshapen by the length of their books,
as by a deficiency in ordinary vanity—they have never
worshipped bodily grace in a manner personal enough to
imitate it; they are neither nervous nor preoccupied,
simply they have never learned. But this is often com-
pensated by a delicacy of smaller movements—gestures
of the hands, inclinations of the head, reclinations of the

whole body. Thus also the engineer: his hands, long-fingered, black-oiled, fluttered beautifully; the movements of his head followed fluently the thoughts of his mind, and even standing his whole body was sitting—he drooped relaxed. He wore dark sunglasses, and perched on his head a blue cap crumpled like a képi from the Crimean war.

He never stopped moving. As he took his glass and first surveyed it, he arched farther backwards, and then as he drank revolved slowly with his lips to the glass, scrutinizing the deep half-circle of sleepers; simultaneously he managed to speak to the barman and wave with his free hand to one of the passengers who was still sitting upright and awake. Now taking his drink he gangled over to this man, and started an intense gesticulated conversation. His body swayed, his hands fluttered, his nose pecked, his eyes rolled. He spoke in French, in either a provençal or Italian dialect. It was difficult to understand all he said—but it had to do with prices, the loan of a gun, and the sale of something he had brought from the mainland. It was plain now that some of his volatility was moved by the common Mediterranean need for commerce, for using each moment as a street-corner; yet this too he managed with a curious distinction. The other man said little, sometimes shrugged his shoulders—his was the situation of the approached. But finally, as if forces had been slowly gathering inside him, he too began to talk, without pause, giving with definition his own idea of the matter; he pointed suddenly to his stomach, and began to talk faster and louder. The engineer opened his arms wide, and managed at the same time to move his shoulders up and down in a series of hopeless shrugs. Impossible, the shoulders said, hopeless. The other man drew from his pocket a note—twenty

9

francs. The shrugging ceased, the engineer took the note
—though indeed still as if there could be no hope, with
down-pressed lips that expressed also something of the
worthlessness of all money—and went shuffling and lurching from the saloon. In a few moments he returned,
carrying bread and a huge dish of soup. The man nodded
and began to eat. Just then, I suppose, my eyes closed and
I was off to sleep.

I was to see much of this engineer, but I did not catch
sight of him again until quite late the next morning.

We put into Ajaccio early—at dawn. The great U-
shaped gulf, long enough to contain two thousand ships,
received us with grey swelling waters, while on either
side the black mountainous coastline raced out to sea;
the first pink light burnt its foundry-glare into a chilled
grey sky, a red glow had already painted the curious Iles
Sanguinaires with the wet of new blood. Those three
sinister islands stood off the cape in a line that seemed to
move. To starboard lay Ajaccio and its few sprouting
palms.

Even at that distance the town, huddled down low
against the dark mountains, looked poor and squalid. And
then, as we neared its long façade, and as the ship seemed
to fly through the water with each flat square-windowed
building marking its speed, that grey light showed
clearly the scabrous texture of each wall, the cracked and
peeling and stained surface of decay. Later, when the sun
had risen and I was warming over a glass of coffee on the
Cours Napoléon, the sun threw into sharper definition the
ulcerous scars, the gutter-soaked patches that smeared
the walls of all those tall barrack-like buildings. The kerbs
had fallen away, sand from the pavements had run in
rivulets out on to the pocked carriageway of this the main
street of the capital; no soft grasses and lichens pursued

such decay, but instead only sand and powdered asphalt giving with their dull ochreous aridity the tone of the town, a town of huge barrack-buildings, dry palms and now leafless plane-trees, of Senegalese troops and occasional statues of Napoléon, of garbage in the streets and a wide main square of sand, of sand and the tricouleur. Two main avenues converged on that immense sandy Place Diamant; along one, the Cours Napoléon, men in many clothes were already sipping their pastis and talking.

I was to know later that in these lines of cafés and bars there was no dancing, only pastis and cards—this was much a garrison town, a port for sailors and land-locked soldiers, upon which one could feel written in the sand and round the monuments and over the acres of blighted plaster the hideous word 'caserne.'

Suddenly I saw again my engineer. He was dressed as before—pale-blue overalls, képi, black glasses; he was thus sharply visible among the khakis and corduroys and greys of the growing crowd. He came gesturing and gangling from the dark door of a bar, as fast as if he had been ejected, holding under one arm a package and in the other the arm of a much shorter and fatter man whom he now dragged at speed along the street. Both men talked fast and without pause, even in their linked position managing to turn their faces close and vehement. They disappeared down one of the steep side streets to the Rue Cardinal Fesch.

Having nothing particular to do but look at the town, I rose and followed. They had chosen this little street for a transaction, and now stood, still gesturing and exploding, between a foot-high mass of cabbage and dung and one of the leaning housewalls with its fat china drainpipe. Then, at some climax, the engineer flourished his parcel, tore off the brown paper, and stood for a moment without

talking, his wide black glasses staring wonderstruck at
the beauty of what was revealed—an American army
jacket and breeches. The smaller man showed instant
disgust, looked up and down the street for something,
anything amusing. But at the same time his left hand
fingered the material of the jacket. The engineer was
talking again. The small man kept shrugging his shoulders. At last, with the downdrawn lips and heavenward
eyes of a dying martyr, he shuffled in his pocket and
brought out some notes. He took the clothes, handed the
engineer the notes. A pause. Then the blue form of the
engineer exploded. He rose on his toes, bending over
the other man like a furious bird, hands wide outstretched like eagle's wings, his nose-beaked head pecking forward with every emphatic word. The smaller man
parried this by staring up at him with his head on one
side, a small smile of unbelief cocking the corner of his
mouth—a sceptic child surveyed his hysterical uncle.
But the volcano proved too much, its force grew until the
smile disappeared. A last shrug of his shoulders. Then
reaching into a pocket that small man drew forth a handful of red cylinders. Cartridges. And these instantly the
engineer took, hiding them, subsiding and simultaneously throwing a hand of affection on his adversary's
shoulder. They then parted on the best, on the face of it,
of terms.

The engineer walked quickly quickly up into the main
street again and disappeared into a bar. I stood waiting
for him to come out—fascinated by such volatility, by
such an exquisite performance of the Mediterranean
pantomime of buy-sell, where the masks of pity and contempt, ennui and obsession, despair and joy, are seen
publicly at their finest extremes. That concession to the
blind eye of the police when one moves off the main street

yet deals in the open! That etiquette of silence while the
other talks! That entrance at a predetermined point of the
score into inspired duet . . . but now the engineer came
bursting out from the bar with a shotgun under his arm.
This altered his manner absolutely, the shotgun slaugh-
tered innocence. With his dark glasses gazing obsessedly
ahead, he strode off to the Place Diamant, whose circuit
he made, keeping to the wall.

Along past the dark yellow military hospital, down the
sea-wall with its row of stunted palms like elephant legs
tufted wearily with green feathers. Along the road that
skirts the side of the gulf, a road marked by a gradual
scarcity of building, a greater decrepitude in the road-
way, by refuse dumps and isolated half-finished concrete
tenements, by bones and offal and driftwood lying puddled
in the red rockpools: and always by the attempt of public
work to be worthy of a capital, but an attempt forlorn,
abandoned at its start, as though some tremendous force
of nature had weighed too heavily down on the hopeless
community of human hearts. A weight of nature was
implemented—for now to either side the majesty of this
island of mountains began to impress itself. Those mountains on the far side of the gulf raced their black humps
far into the sea, snow on their peaks glittered like sugar
in the sun, pockets of poisonous wool drifted longingly
across the valley cuts; while to the right of our road rose
the near slopes of the maquis, small ascending mountains
thickly covered with aromatic scrub, so that they looked
smooth and furry, like convulsed green baize.

The engineer walked fast, bouncing on his toes, throwing his elbows back and jolting like a professional walker.
His head under that képi now searched the terrain to the
right: he might have been looking for one of the few
scattered villas that straggled about the slope. On he

went. We passed a sudden, then endless cemetery of bright stone house-tombs, each built much more stably than the houses back in the capital—sealed evidences of Corsican pride and familiarity with death. Abruptly the cemetery ceased and the road grew houseless and wild, with no embankment against the gulf, and growing on either side wet green cactus studded with yellow flowers. The Iles Sanguinaires moved like a line of ships in the distance. The maquis rose unwalled on our right.

The engineer stopped, glanced keenly up the hill-side. Very quickly he took cartridges from his pocket—I saw them flash red as they were snapped away into the gun. Then he was off climbing up the steep, rough incline. He climbed like a frog, spreading his hands and long thin legs to grasp branches and to grip the greyish boulders, thrusting forward his body against the gradient. It was hardly prudent to follow him immediately—on a road my presence might have been coincidental, but on the pathless maquis not. I waited.

In fact, was it prudent to follow him at all? There he went, purposely armed, intent on some firm direction— probably some goat-herd's shack, some outlying cottage. The morning paper had already told me that the day before, yesterday, there had been a shooting in the main café in Ajaccio—a husband seated with his wife and another man had suddenly risen to his feet and shot this other man bluntly in the stomach. And some time in the recent past a night-club manager had shot a sailor in the neck for disturbing his orchestra with an impromptu on the accordion. There had been bullet holes in the mirror of another café. And the Corsican is renowned for his history of proud summary justice. Whatever then the engineer would do might involve me, if I remained so close—either as an accomplice, or as a witness. Or the engineer himself would shoot me as a spy? However . . . the affair was too mature to abandon. Besides, we were in the country, with no easy diversions. So I decided to climb up into the maquis at a parallel distance from the engineer, to climb faster and thus higher than him, so that I could look down on his direction. With the cover afforded by scrub it would be fairly simple to remain unobserved—and my suit was grey, whereas his was bright-washed blue.

A sweaty climb under the rising sun. The maquis is a strange mixture of hard and soft things, of sudden aromatic carpets of herb, of eruptions of hard grey boulders, of soft arbutus and cystus, and then of spiny cactus. But mostly it feels soft, looking so moss-green, the hill-top a high ridge of green fur against the blue sky; the air smells sweet as so many odorous plants are crushed by the heel. Though it was steep and tiring, the climb was a joy: a sense of great freedom among such windwashed luxuriance in the warm winter sun made me forget the engineer. Or postpone him. But arrived at last at my eminence I took cover, and looked round. He was nowhere to be seen. I felt in my haversack for the glasses, and then began to scrutinize carefully the intricate shrub.

No sound. No movement over all the expanse of rolling lichenous sward—only sometimes the silent glint of a bird skimming the low branches, or curving up suddenly like a feather kicked on hot air. The arm of scented green stretched out to sea—for this was the thick upper arm of a cape—and on either side extended, far and near, the sea. No forest murmur here, no trees to move in those slight breezes that fanned the two shores: it was deadly set, like a painted plaster model. In ancient times pilots knew this island from a distance because of the perfume that drifted far out over the sea, a perfume of flowering shrub that caused those ancient oarsmen to call it the Scented Isle. But now it was winter, warm but flowerless —and still.

The black sockets of my binoculars traversed slowly. Up the slight hills, down suddenly into overgrown ravines, past a ruined goatherd's hut, over a circle of stones that had once based a sheep-pen or a Genoese watch-tower. Suddenly I saw the peaked blue képi, a pale-blue tropical bird above a bush of myrtle. The man was crouched, moving sideways with the gun stealthily creeping to his shoulder. The dark glasses were fixed emotionless and ruthless on something at the centre of a circle he was making; my glasses were focused clear on those dark others. A slow movement, trying to make no sound—and in the binoculars there was an augmented silence. Over all, the immense quiet of the day.

It was difficult to move the binoculars off him. At such a moment he might have made some decisive move, disappearing into the bush. But at length, as his movements seemed to remain so steady, I shifted those black circles carefully across. There was nothing.

I searched in vain—for a hut, for some other man's movement, for the movement of a branch that might show up some other man. But there was nothing—and I knew by the direction of his glasses that he was anticipating no long shot. Whoever he was after lay close. No movement, no life in that scrub—only suddenly a pinpoint of colour that intensified the strange stillness. A robin sat on one of the branches. Its orange breast caught the sunlight, it was opening and shutting its beak as if trying to sing— for of course no sound came.

It did not seem possible. At first I discarded the idea. But as the minutes passed the truth emerged; irrefutable and, through the glasses, of strange isolated power. The

16

engineer was stalking that robin. I switched the glasses to and fro, certainly the gun's barrel was trained on the little bird's level. But—why not shoot? Then, as the engineer quietly lowered his head to the gunsight, it was plain to see why he had held his fire. He had been moving round *behind the robin*. Some deep amazing instinct had instructed him to shoot this little bird in the back.

For a long time the scene stayed fixed. That man's head was now lowered to the sights, so that the peak of his pale képi ran parallel with the gun. It looked more than ever like a bird, or like some false effigy of a bird, a pointed blue-beaked thing like a carnival mask, like the cruel disguise of some grotesque bird-watcher's hood. And a few yards across the scented foliage, whose every fragile leaf was set so still, there sat the other bird, the real little bird. With its back turned. So that the two made a silent unmoving procession of birds. Not a leaf shivered; they were like leaves seen on a cinema film, bright and unreal. The figure in the képi seemed cast in wax. Only the little bird's mouth could be seen faintly moving— perhaps eating. That small movement only accentuated the silence, as though the bird were singing without sound.

Suddenly it rose in the air, blasted by a sudden wind, and then with scattering wings dropped. At the same time the foliage behind shivered. Then a drift of smoke came, and a prancing blue figure—just as the echoing shot-sound cracked as if behind my ear. I kept the binoculars fixed, my two holes of vision showed the blue figure thrashing excitedly in the tangled shrub, eagerly pouncing then lifting aloft, with a backward-leaning motion of triumph, a small furry ball of grey and orange.

Some hours later, having lunched in Ajaccio, I saw him again. He was talking to two elderly Corsicans. He held

in his hand a small bunch of little birds—three at least
were robins. These he brandished in the faces of the two
old men, who seemed annoyed and looked pointedly
away. This time I determined to hear what was said. They
were standing at a point that I could approach without
seeming inquisitive.

They were standing near to the old fountain in the
barrack wall. Here, in a stone recess behind an iron
railing, was a place where old men habitually forgath-
ered. Such old men stood there for hours, leaning on the
iron railing, gossiping, gazing at the passers-by of the
Place Diamant and past them across the sandy waste to
the leprous line of houses stretching to the gulf-wall, at
the gulf and its sombre mountains beyond. The engineer
and his two acquaintances were standing outside the
railing. It seemed that only the poorer went inside, men
who had had their day; and somehow they must have
formed a focal point for street standing, because it was
around here that a ragged crowd always loitered and
talked. This I now joined.

After a few hours on the island my understanding of
the patois was growing clearer. They spoke Corsican—
not the romance language of the midi, but a mixture of
French and Genoese. The two old men were pure
islanders. They wore the wide curl-brimmed black hats,
the long jackets of chestnut brown corduroy, the bright-
scarlet cummerbunds that still form a much-worn national
dress among the older country-people. And Ajaccio,
besides being a caserne, still retained some of the feeling
of a large market town, it attracted people from the hills,
the farmers, the millers, the sons of labourers and gentlemen and bandits. These old two, with their lean high
cheekbones and their draped moustaches, were Corsicans of
old stock, men of the bandit days. Their bearing was proud.

Such pride, such granite unconcern must have proved a formidable barrier to the engineer's commerce. But a barrier that perhaps he welcomed, as many small illnesses are welcomed, for the passionate pain they provoke. There was no doubt that he was now in pain. He had pushed his dark glasses on to his forehead, agonized eyebrows reached up to them like the stretched legs of frogs, his dark searching eyes glittered, his lips seemed to move in a motion faster than the flow of words—and all the time that small wedge of little birds fluttered between his mouth and the stern eyes of the two disapproving old men. The old men—perhaps owners of a restaurant, perhaps of good wives—were potential buyers of the robins. One of them said:

"I have offered you six francs the bird."

He said this without vehemence, as having stated not a price but some patriarchal law. He said nothing further, only pulled slowly at a tooth under his moustache. The engineer burst into an appeal of despair—for ten francs the bird. Ten francs! Ten small francs for the most savoury, the delicious little bird! Shot even that morning, fresh from eating the odorous maquis—the exquisite bird of the red throat!

But obduracy had hardened in the veins of those old men. Many Mediterranean peoples buy, sell, bargain, run after coins bright and round as their sun, run after them without shame and with laughter, even without avarice and only as a reasonable means to an end. These Corsicans are different. Centuries of fighting against imperialists from the mainlands, against Spain and France and always Genoa, have welded them into firm communities, groups of the family and of the village and of the island. Their need was always to be self-provident, independent in their mountains and thence independent

in their hearts. That which they own they give freely—
but they will fight bitterly if it is snatched by force.
Such a pride does not allow them to bargain. They state
their view, their fair price. It is the last word.

Infuriating for the sinuous engineer. This one was now
driven by his sunsoaked frenzy into a beatification that
soon rose far beyond his wares, rose from praising the
dead bird to a lyric of the bird alive, the bird he had shot,
but of whose life and beauty he was deeply aware. Of
course, he exaggerated:

"Fine, the little rouge-gorge! High in the maquis
she sits, her breast shines like the red arbutus. Small,
yes, but up there in the green it is the only little person
that is alive—like a mouse she darts among the low
branches."

As he spoke his eyes rolled, his fingers played with
air as lightly as birds' wings—this shooter of birds in the
back. But transported now, it was plain that while killing
birds he loved them, or knew their live mystery, their
freedom. I who while eating flesh condemn any joy in its
killing was astounded—it had never occurred to me that
you could love these things exactly at the same time as
killing, that in fact the processes of loving life and
killing it for one's own survival could occur in the same
brain at the same time, fully, without the trammellings
of pity. To all this the old men iust nodded. They too
knew.

"There was the sky, blue and wide, the great sky, and
up flew the little bird, its red breast shining in the sun,
I saw the red, I aimed. . ."

Of course he never saw the red. Nor did he see what I
saw—thrushes I had eaten at lunch, little naked birds
served whole and still on thick toast. Birds featherless
as fledglings, with their beaks and big-lidded eyes shut

and saurian, baby pterodactyls. A delicacy, for their flesh was nurtured on the aromatic scrub. Others in the restaurant lifted the birds with their fingers and picked with their teeth at the heads.

"I sprang forward! I picked her up, and she was still warm. See, only this morning, warm and fresh from the herbs of the maquis . . ."

And there he was tacked back again on to his selling course. The flight of fancy was over. But it had been real. He was no poet, he was an engineer and apart from his looks a not uncommon one. Yet, here he was one of a curious breed—the breed of the loving hunter. No regrets, he faced up to the cruelty of life and lived his part of it; and he loved life. An æsthete of the open field, he saw his prey as a thing of beauty. But he saw it according to the scale of his own animality, not with sentiment as a fellow creature. It could only have been love that gave him such joy in killing. He cared much more than on the score of prowess. He cared much more than an ordinary lover of beauty—the debased æsthete who is held to be all heart and sympathy, but who so often becomes the most intolerant of men, a creature refined beyond generous living. But here was the predatory æsthete, a fine mind if a dark one.

However—his words were now of no use—the thoughtful patriarchs rebutted him with their pride. They made no further offer, but simply let him speak himself back into silence. As for him—perhaps he had the whole afternoon to spare and a whole town of buyers to try, or he was defiant on his own terms. In any case, he suddenly turned away, and with a brief word of parting went striding fast round the corner into the afternoon crowd of the Cours Napoléon. I followed. Once round the corner he stopped, undecided. He was still quivering with his extraordinary vehemence, more alive and alight than ever. He paused, one could hear him raging inside: 'Where now, where now with my little robins?' Suddenly he decided; in his awkward but swiftly efficient way he darted away into the crowd, into the mixed moving mass of corduroy and dark blue and Latin black and Senegalese red and all the patched-up khaki that made the fashionable throng of this capital street. He disappeared. But I was to see him frequently throughout the afternoon—before the tumultuous evening ever began.

In such a small town it is difficult to avoid meeting again such an acquaintance—particularly as my own afternoon was spent wandering and looking. Thus I saw him in the market down by the quay, out by the railway station with its earnest small trains winding off up the mountains to the old capital of Corte, in a cool stone restaurant spacious with pots of plants and lean tailless dogs, in a bar whose fixtures were of the Empire's gold and mahogany, in one of the cavernous dark shops sacked with grain and pasta. Each time he was bargaining, brandishing the robins. Not only with the imperturbable Corsican, but with other more vociferous Latins. As the hours passed, so the feathers of the little birds grew fluffed and scragged. But it seemed no one would pay his price; perhaps he deceived himself by applying the higher prices of the mainland to the simpler island economy. It seemed, at all costs, such a small transaction; but the engineer had plainly become obsessed. The transaction had become more important than the profit. Besides, many other small deals could be seen loitering round those streets—there was one tall Senegalese walking slowly from restaurant to restaurant like a priest in his red fez, a single blue-black crayfish weaving its worried feelers from his purple-black hand.

Towards four o'clock the sun grew milky and disappeared, massive clouds came lowering in from the sea. The ochreous town grew pale beneath a giant darkness. An hour later, the storm had still not broken. Still it massed strength, piling up weight upon weight of cloud, darkness upon darkness. It was about then, at five o'clock, that I noticed a crowd taking a direction: everyone seemed to be moving down from the Cours and the big Place towards the harbour, in fact towards another square enclosing yet another statue of Napoléon and at the same time the Hôtel de Ville.

It was outside this pillared and balconied seat of government that a large crowd now collected. A newly elected deputy was formally taking over his office. Ajaccio had assembled to acclaim him. Now they waited, strolled, chattered, milled; a feeling of storm, of tense expectation, of suppressed revelry tautened the air—and suddenly all the electric lights were switched on. Wired among the branches of the plane and palm trees covering this little square, the yellow bulbs blazed gaudily, lit up the autumn leaves, cut themselves bright against the slate-dark sky above. Through the tall window of the balcony a glittering glass chandelier shone, telling of rich official pomp, of soft ambassadorial feet within.

All Ajaccio! That hot, seedy crowd gathered to the centre of their sun-soaked town with not much more purpose than just to gather, to stir into life. Throughout those latitudes townspeople gathered for the evening parade, for the strolling and passing and turning about in their thousand twilit squares; but this was more— some came with political feeling, others stirred patrioti-

cally, for all there was the expectation of an 'occasion'!
So they stood about on the sandy ground under the plane-
trees and palms, all eyes on the central yellow building
with its chandelier, with its draped swathe of tricouleur,
with its ionic portico and its old red carpet frayed and
holed. Blue-uniformed cadets lined the entrance. A loudspeaker attached to the balcony roared out music from a
gramophone—Viennese waltzes, giddying javas, jazz.
That loudspeaker seemed to be made all of wire, it grated
so. And so also the bell that suddenly chimed five from
the clock-tower—a thin wiry bell shrill above the metal
music; and the wired feeling of the electric lights among
the branches—through the warm air all these makeshift
wires galvanized the night. The yellow tower steadily
grew paler against the monstrous cloud looming indigo
above; soon its stucco seemed to shine against so much
darkness; then, from far across the mountains, there
flickered sudden violet flashes, like shadows of light
growing huge and as swiftly gone—the pagan lightning
crossed the mountains with angry leaps, bewildered the
electric night.

Such giant violet flickerings made the little square
smaller, exaggerated the dreadful clarity of those high
wide mountain spaces above. The town huddled closer;
nursing its shoddiness; boasting its claim with bright-
yellow bulbs and loud music. And several little boys were
already letting off ground fireworks, so that crimson and
green flares began to colour the crowd, casting fantastic
shadows, while small drifts of smoke drifted a light fog
here and there.

Napoléon stood moveless in white marble, encircled
in his grove of withered palms. Four lions slobbered at
his feet, their mouths green with moss over which slow
water trickled; it seemed that these lions, snub-faced as

pekingese, dropped their saliva as the townsfolk themselves spat, with no ejaculatory effort—it was too hot—
only leaning their heads aside and letting the saliva fall.
By the railings of this statue a small dark man in khaki
plus-fours was tearing up long strips of white paper for
makeshift confetti; past him walked two fine dark
beauties, black-eyed nubiles of the south, their hair a
chemical gold; a group of middle-aged men passed—
grey sweaters, brown boots, black hats, silver bristles,
striped dusty trousers—and their women with them,
shapeless in black; a muscle-chested brown young man in
a striped singlet, with a white cap set squarely over his
head—the cap had a great white button round as his
roving eye; two naval airmen, quiet in their disciplined
nonentity, their fear; a large girl with high flat cheekbones like her thick-boned ankles, as if an olive-skinned
Swede; youths slouching quickly, swinging their arms,
kicking at odd stones, vigorous and laughing braggishly
at each other; a man in khaki breeches and woollen
stockings, a motor-racer's leather cap flapping over his
ears; Senegalese; Tunisians; Italians; French—and
suddenly, thin and knobbly in pale blue came jerking
along that engineer! Now his glasses were off. He still
held in his hand the bunch of robins.

As he came round the railings and took a course diag-
onally across the square, his sharp inquisitive face pecked
in every direction, his eyes darted everywhere—no one
in that whole crowd could have escaped him. Then, as
usual, he disappeared into a bar.

This bar lay down towards the sea end of the square,
whose lower end was open to the quay. It was a cavern
bar, with a wide opening like half a huge egg. When I
came in, the engineer had already engaged himself
heavily with another man, a short man (they all looked

short against his long figure). This man wore a leather
motor-coat with a fur collar, American army boots and
breeches, a beret. As always the blue képi was lowered
down at his face, before which swung the robins. However, this time there was a difference. The engineer now
held a glass of pastis in his free hand. Moreover, the
shorter man had also taken a glass of pastis, and perhaps
more than one. He hardly played his part in the discussion of the robins correctly, he was unserious, he
smiled, he laughed, he interrupted the engineer to lay
an arm on his shoulder, protesting his delight in seeing
his old friend the engineer, declaiming and pouting his
manly love with a puffing of cheeks and a bracing of
biceps. Worse, he praised the robins.

"Oui, mon Dominique, fine birds! Beauties!"

"Eh?"

"Beauties! And good shooting, Dominique mon
cher."

"Ah. Mm. But you are right. You see them, you know.
There's no more to be said. I'll———"

"Yes, old fellow, good shooting. Dominique knows a
rifle. Remember, Dominique, the night at Porto when
———"

"For you especially, for you my old friend, I offer them
for only twelve francs the bird. Twelve! No more."

"———the night you engaged the good macaronis———"

"Listen, Emilio, the birds———"

"Ten macaronis and a beautiful machine gun, phat-
ta-ta-tat. And my Dominique with his old rifle, jumping
about in the dark, firing from here, there and everywhere
like twenty men. By God, you could not blame them."

"Emilio, I shot them this morning, five of them."

"Macaronis?"

"Macaronis hell—*red-breasts!*"

26

"Ah, the beauties."

"Emilio—ten francs the bird."

But already Emilio was signing for two more pastis making large round generous signs with his muscular hands, so that two double glasses of the milk-white absinthe faced them on the zinc. With an abrupt gesture of impatience the engineer tossed back his first glass, then took up the new one. For a moment he said nothing, but looked down darkly at the robins. Emilio went on to talk of old times in the maquis. Behind them a weak electric light cast the shadows of its bracket across a wall alive with menacing shapes, giant brown sunflowers on an oil-green paper. The paper had been laid over previous embossed decorations, and now bulged and receded, rose and fell without moving. Two bicycles stood against a wicker table. Outside, through the dark arch of the entrance, the Place des Palmiers showed brightness and movement, the crowd was still growing, the flare and smoke of more fireworks veiled it with a sense of furnaces, of carnival. Music echoed across the warm air like the throbbing steam-music of a fair. Emilio had begun to sing a marching song.

The engineer suddenly emptied his glass and called for two more. He frowned, and as if making a decision emptied also his new glass of pastis. Then, at the top of his voice, he began trying again to sell the birds to Emilio. He shook the birds savagely. One or two small feathers floated down to the wine-stained floor. But Emilio went on singing, now with closed eyes, feet marching up and down, his forearm bunched to slope an imaginary rifle. So that the engineer Dominique's voice rose also louder, he began to rave. I moved away to the arched door. Emilio, who was neither acting nor insensitive that he was being spoken to, occasionally broke off in the middle

27

of his song to pat the birds and enquire after Dominique's family.

"And your *mother*? How is your *mother*? Lola, how is *Lola*? A big girl? Beautiful?"

"All their lives they have been feeding on the maquis, the herbs. Emilio, eight francs, you rob me."

Emilio had turned away and was paying much more—sixty francs—for two large pastis. As indeed previously the engineer had done—he who had spent a day trying to sell five birds for about fifty francs. But it was the transaction, not the profit. But now suddenly the arm holding the little birds drooped low, another blue arm reached out to Emilio's neck—and softly, with an oddly open mouth, the engineer began to croon. He sang in a sweet tenor the same song as Emilio, holding tremulously on to the sustained notes. His whole rapacious face took on the look of a thin old woman transported by sentimental thoughts; now wide open, his lips disappeared thinly stretched to show—a shock—that he had no teeth. The black hole of a mouth looked like one black sunglass.

I could hear gusts of their talk—for every so often they stopped singing and, embracing, exchanged greetings and reminiscence. The glasses of pastis, strong drink of wormwood that first tastes weak, came and went. They grew more and more friendly. Sometimes one said:

"Eh, Dominique!"

While the other, leaning back the better to survey his old friend, would intone his reply with a frown of loving bravado:

"Emilio!"

Outside, the tension had reached some sort of a climax —the appearance of the deputy seemed to be due. The crowd had grown thick round the portico of the hotel, I could see the brass instruments of a band flashing dully about the bottom steps. From this centre the square beneath those trees was forested with groups of people, black against the lights, against the whitish firework smoke. Not a crowd dense as in a great city, but a large crowd dispersed, populating the whole square. The plane branches and their dried November leaves made a ceiling of the electric light, such foliage looked papery, like illuminated theatrical trees. Such a ceiling a few feet above the people's heads existed throughout all the twenty-four hours of all southern towns—in daytime the leaves enclosed with shade the pavement, while all light and energy lay high in the sunlit air above; at night at the same level the shade became reversed, the dark inactive night stretched its black vacuum above, while beneath the same low ceiling all was light and movement.

"Chestnut cakes at Piana—remember? Fresh from the wood!"

"The Rizzanese—a real river that, fine cold water!"

> "Ah! le petit vin blanc—
> Qu'on boit sous les tonnelles."

Now they were singing together the generous little waltz-tune. Their movement as they swayed, as the engineer beat time with his bunch of birds, seemed, with the sound of their singing, to fill the dark little bar. Outside night had not yet fallen. There was still in the air, besides the occasion and the music and the fireworks, that excitement, that air of prelude that charges the twilight air with promises of night. Against now a sky the colour of dark iron, the façades of the buildings shone incandescently white, pearl-coloured, pale as bone. Only the decorated Hôtel de Ville broke the regularity of these square façades with their black regular windows; the Hôtel de Ville with its clock-tower, its coat-of-arms, its ionic pillars, its balcony, its brave draping of the blue, white and red flag of France.

"Emilio, old friend, listen! A mark of esteem, in honour of our meeting, in celebration of the Deputy. His Honour. Emilio—a gift—I *give* you the birds!"

"Uh?"

"The birds, my little robins! I give them to you."

"What?"

"For nothing!"

"Eh?"

"There, take them."

"But . . . well, many thanks. Many, many thanks."

"Ah!"

"But——"

"Yes?"

"But Dominique, my Dominique——"

" Ah! le petit vin blanc."

"But Dominique, I cannot take them. I must pay. Here, fifty francs."

"No!"

"Forty francs."

"You insult me!"

"Take twenty."

"If you insist."

"There!"

"Now. Permit me to offer you a pastis."

A murmur came from the crowd, and this rose to a shout. Behind me the singing stopped. Those two had heard the shout. Now with cries of 'the Deputy!' they were running past me and out through the door. Through the crowd they dodged, the long engineer first, Emilio on shorter legs zigzagging behind. They ran like children, like enthused students—not worrying whom they bumped, laughing and letting arms and jacket flap wildly.

The engineer's arms were free, he no longer held his robins.

Over by the steps now everyone and everything had collected. A passage had been cleared by cadets and police. Down this the old red carpet, dusty and holed, stretched its royal channel. As it finished, so there began the band, an elderly and jovial group of players in assorted clothes—from plus-fours to breeches of corduroy—but each wearing a dark jacket and an old peaked cap. They looked like railwaymen; but each held proudly his brass or silver instrument, and one man was already bent backwards against the weight of his big bass drum. Several small boys ran about in the aisle carrying white boards on sticks. On the boards were written 'Vive la Republique!' and 'Criez le 20 Octobre!' And on all sides the crowd, old and young, men and women, pressed forward, singing, jostling, shouting, and all waving long strips of white paper.

A brief hush. Movements occurred at the back of the hall inside. The loudspeaker music abruptly stopped. The band raised their instruments to their lips. And on the steps there emerged the deputy and a little procession of officials.

At the same moment the loudspeaker above the balcony burst into music louder, faster, wilder than any before. But it was not the Marseillaise, nor a Corsican anthem, nor any martial song at all. There came the hot thunderous cacophony of negroes—'Washboard Blues!' Simultaneously the band began to play—but only the loud thumping of the big drum could be heard above the loudspeaker. The procession began to move down the steps and away. Instantly—for the crowd stood only three feet off on either side—they were mobbed. The air flew with white paper strips. A hundred arms reached forward to touch the deputy. Shouts, cheers, wild whistling. From all sides a battery of fireworks burst—green, yellow, Mephistophelian red. Through all this, the procession struggled away as it could, fighting through the smoke and colour and laughter, then turned sharply right into the Rue Fesch. The famous old street, narrow and winding, was filled to the walls of its tall houses with a jostling mass. All along its serpentine way the people crammed. Away in front, growing dimmer, the beat of the big drum echoed. After it, flexing like a dragon, wound the procession of all Ajaccio. Banners swayed, arms tossed hats high, the dragon swarmed waddling on a thousand unseen legs.

Then I saw for the last time that tall blue képi—higher than the rest of the crowd but caught in it, laughing and fighting and struggling as he was borne along, as now he receded from me, dragged away, drowned it seemed in the moving swelling devouring sea, the sea of hats, caps, fezzes, hands, arms, faces. . .

I walked back to the bar. There on the floor half beneath the wicker table lay the little robins, ruffled, deflated, their skinny eyelids closed tight, their short beaks shut, and all around like bright puffs of dust the small feathers.

POSEIDON'S DAUGHTER

~

THE hour before dawn. A wind blew in, softly and cool, from the wide dusk-blue Tyrrhenian. Such a light breath of wind could properly be called a zephyr; it came from the narcissus islands lying out in that old sea whose blue hymen was ploughed by the keels of the first sailors. It breathed in over a rocky land that must remain perpetually ancient, and of Greece; a land echoing still the graven Greek sigh, that sigh for a haven, wine, oxen, the wood-fire on the beach. This zephyr then: it blew in suddenly through the wide white-painted arches of Pietro's verandah, fluttering slightly the leaves of a creeper-vine, kissing the erect cactus, fanning the airy stone room within. In different ways it startled the two people silently occupied in that room.

Pietro was standing naked, adjusting the strings of a bathing slip, a triangle at his loins. When the wind touched him, he looked up quickly to the greying light; the wind carried a message from the sea to his fisherman's senses, he listened at it, judging whether this was the herald of greater winds and surf or no more—and what in fact it seemed to be—than the last breath of night expiring before the South Italian day. Then, with a sharp eye of care, he looked over to the figure of his wife lying sprawled and stifled in the bed by the wall. She stirred uneasily, grunted, twisted her tortured arm farther behind her neck—the wind must have touched her like a cold hand, a shiver in the hot bones of fever. How hot the bed looked, the only thing of cloth in the bare stone-domed room. Pietro stood for a moment looking at her. She

breathed too quickly, straining at something in the dark
mind of her sleep. He knew that this might become some
sort of a climax; but the illness had now continued for so
long a time, with so many false crises, so many periods of
subsidence and relapse, that his concern for her had
become amorphous, he could no longer define his care.
Nothing could be done but wait—and fish for food, good
food fresh from the sea.

He noticed, in that colourless light, that her face was
smeared with black mascara and red lip-rouge. She would,
then, have been up in the night, sleep-walking, painting
her face in some dream. He cursed himself once more for
being so deep a sleeper. He never knew all she did during
those rigid midnight errands, those ghost-walks out-
wardly balanced and serene . . . but moved by what
tempests of restlessness within? However—she did nothing dangerous, no harm had been done as far as
he knew. He smiled now suddenly at the red and
black smears on her sleeping face—a ribald pattern, a
caligraphy of debauch. He smiled—then wondered
what longing had set her down at the dressing-table,
what pathetic wish for other days of health and dancing.
He turned impatiently to the verandah. Useless to waste
time.

Out on the verandah he found his mask and harpoon
and again paused—to look out over the wide sea below,
to listen at the air for the weather of the fish, to note fine
rippling lines engraved on the calm depth now indigo
below the pale-green trellis of vine-leaves. On this scene
of grape and saltwater, of the wedding of opposing land
and sea—he felt abruptly imposed the image of his
wife's face. A South Italian of generations back, she
was pale-skinned, grey-eyed, freckled round the eyes
like a doe; these strange textures had never ceased to

surprise, for the people of the coast were dark-skinned and arabic. But in itself such a contrast symbolized the ancient littoral that had first known the Greeks, then the Romans, the armoured fair-skinned Normans, the strong blood of Arab pirates, the Aragonese from Spain; and that finally had become part of modern Italy. A complicated strain: though still no stronger influence remained than that ancient one of Greece, the fishing town took its name direct from great-bearded Poseidon.

Inconsequently it seemed, as he stood there naked and motionless as a god, the silver staff of his harpoon in one hand, the black mask hanging like fish-skin at his side, this man Pietro thought of his own name—Piotr. An image of the letters in his mind made his lips whisper the sound, a whispering heard from a great distance of years. Neither magical nor heartbreaking—this music of the old name: for the new name had grown upon him as pleasantly as had the character of his place of exile. Though a certain sunlight irradiates most memories of youth, the sun of this Tyrrhenian beach, which had been his home now for twenty years, had drowned in its great potency all other sunlights. Perhaps a northern freshness could be remembered in the glassy clarity of that boy-hood sunlight on the Baltic; but the warmth, the long warm drenching of a palpable southern sun, had long ago enervated and then in its dark way revitalized his energies: clear comparisons had died. From the grey waters of Finland twenty years before to this ancient beach of the Greeks. Another ingredient thus to the mixture, another ingredient to be digested in the ancient mystery of sea and vine, old colloquy loved by the first sailors. He turned and walked down the steepstone steps to the alley outside.

35

His way led downward steeply in a lane walled by stone houses. The lane was itself made of steps, so that the whole might have been carved from the rock itself; but this was illusory, the fishing houses were built in tiers rising above one another, the steps set there to form the most rapid street to that essential beach below. Each wall was washed white, the steps remained grey; many of the houses stood holed by the dark crescents of saracen arches, most carried not tiled roofs but shallow domes of stone. Such domes spoke again of arab influences—but also they had been adopted as a means to save timber; there was little timber in that region of rocks and bush-plant. And all these stone elements and the firm and varied geometry of walls and buttresses suggested that the whole might be carved like a giant honeycomb from the solid rock; sometimes a thick arch crossed the lane, supporting two leaning houses; sometimes an outcrop wall widened towards the ground, slab-cut like a white cheese. All was of stone, with here and there in the steep descent patches of green vine, spiked cactus, or a sudden rich spraying of white and purple flowers. Once a larger house, a villa, revealed its cosseting of purple bougainvillea, a luxuriance rescued from vulgarity by some resemblance to glazed flowers painted on tiles. So through the narrow channels of winding stone Pietro descended, moving slowly in the grey-blue lightening dusk, half-eager for the sea, half-drawn to the house above where no one watched over the lonely fever-bed.

He came out from the conglomerate of houses straight on to a beach of rough grey sand. A small movement was apparent; two or three solitary dark shapes of fishermen walked to and from their boats, carrying tackle and jars— the residue of a night's fishing by lamp-flare. Otherwise the beach was deserted. Behind, there rose the almost

perpendicular circle of mountains, now dark and tremendously silent, dark as the black-faced charcoal burn-
ers who inhabited their rugged crests. To sea it was
lighter, not yet coloured by the sun; but brilliant, for the
water caught in its imperceptible movements whatever
light there was. A deserted dawn—rinsed clear of contemporary life, ancient and heavy with premonition. Such
a premonition—which Pietro felt strongly—might have
been that which seems to heave in all old things, less a
forewarning than a command to remember what powers
once resided there; or it might have been more simply the
animal message of the fading night—the warning that
day and new action are about to begin; but to that man,
standing now on the wet sand by the sea's edge, feeling
the night-cooled water fresh over his toes, it was more
easily translated as a personal warning, so that he felt
uneasy again about the house alone and unprotected above.
Should he have left her alone? At such a possible crisis?
Was there not still time to postpone this hunting in the
water and climb back to watch over her? But the hunting
had to be done.

Food was vital. The people about knew he had little
money and often offered him part of their catch; but they
themselves were poor: he had taken already more than
his conscience liked, it was important to fish for himself.
He had no boat. The harpoon was his only precarious
weapon. He paused wondering, looked up at the house,
then out to the islands. The hump-backed whale-shapes
swam breeding their old superstitions, demarcating the
premonitory air. Islands animate the sea that lies between
them and the shore: they alone state that the channel
between is not endless sea but drowned land populated
with things that at any time might rise, seaweed creatures and briny gods whose form they the islands them-

37

selves seem to shadow in their monstrous bulk. In that moment of facing the sea during which the sea-going man pauses, however many times he might have paused before, and surveys with virgin interest the mystery, Pietro sensed deeply the demarcation to the islands. Then he spat, threw away his cigarette, and waded in.

Up to his chest he stopped, wettened his mask, fixed the black rubber across his face. The breathing pipe and its cork float hung like a strange sea-flower at his ear; then, shoulders submerged, only the head remained, a strange inquisitive projection from that flat water, with its glassy face and gleaming black head like the snub face of a serpentine phantom cocked up in periscope search. Then this head rolled over and assumed the sea, while the straight body rose behind, and with propeller legs and a slow scything of arms moved easily and swiftly towards the deeper water.

As his feet left the shingled sand and he felt the freedom of the water, as the cool water flowed back past him and the frothy wake broke easily at his threshing feet, there was no more question of the sea's adversity—borne on it and in it he was instantly part of that sea, familiar, and guarded safe. The element took his mind, the buoyant clear water refreshed minerally his body, his eyes gazing down through the glass mask entered into a world of different texture and light, an absolute world of water so delineated by the surface ceiling that the air-world might have been experienced months, not only a moment, previously. The prospect now was purple and greenish, lit by a strange brilliant light, as though somewhere in the distance bright tubes of gas might be burning. Too deep to see the bottom. He knew by this that it was time to turn. His destination lay by a rocky promontory to the

right of the small bay. He could swim laterally towards
this pincer-point of rock. It was unusual to find large
tunny so close in to shore; but there were cuttle-fish, and
with luck a parent octopus whose thick tentacles could
provide a good few meals.

Surfacing then his head to judge the direction, he
turned over, and for some seconds drifted on his back,
weaving his hands slowly like fins. Eyes above water, it
seemed in its turn that the underwater element had never
existed. There again lay the tiered honeycomb of houses,
the green-domed church, the crescent beach of drawn-up
boats; also much of the care of the world, much of the
landed care that leaves the spirit as the body is given to
the water. From where he swam he could see the vertical
town in longer perspective, how it clustered up neatly in
the concave mountain hollow. He noted too the few
modern interpolations, now so reduced in size as to appear
more than usually insignificant—a short line of bathing
huts, isolated like sentry-boxes with nothing to guard,
with no direction, empty; one beach-parasol, sprouting
lonely like a dark fungus by the water's edge; a varnished
motor-boat glinting like brittle-bad furniture among the
weather-washed paint of the fishing-boats. Such anachronisms propped themselves uselessly against the granite
sand, the ancient reality of rock and vine and embedded
house.

How living was such an antiquity! How haunted with
the dead, how alive with their legend! A mixed legend,
various as the races that had woven it. But underneath the
many tales a common seed lay. Some accounts, for instance, told that a pirate ship, driven along the coast by
terrible storms, had come abreast of the bay, and had
heard through the raging wind a voice crying 'Posa!
Posa!' Obeying this instruction to set down, they had

driven inbeach and landed on what had proved a safe haven. There on the beach they had found the figure of a Madonna. To this instantly they had attributed the strange voice of their salvation. In gratitude they had erected a shrine—and that was the origin of the village Positano. Other accounts told of a pirate ship bearing down armed to sack the small fishing village—whereat a voice from the sea had cried 'Posa! Posa!' and instantly like a stone the pirate ship had sunk straight to the bottom of the bay. To this day, in crevices along the walls of the narrow streets, shrines to the Virgin of the Sea may be seen: Positano's saint is a Virgin Mary rising from the sea. Yet long before this someone had called a more ancient settlement after the sea-god Poseidon. And there again . . . Poseidon came from the sea. And some sources suggest that the narcissus islands a few kilometres to sea were the islands from which the Sirens sang to Ulysses. The sea-born sirens too . . . thus, whatever the form, *something* came out of the sea. A warning. A god. A song. The beach had always looked to the sea for its terrible help.

Pietro turned and faced down into the water again, swimming with an easy roll towards the promontory of rocks. As he swam, the legend thrummed with the water in his ears, repeating and repeating. And at the same time the first light must have struck from above—a rosy dawn-glow that hit into the water and deepened the purple glow beneath; but this he did not see, for his face was pressed down into the water—he saw only the brightening of the neon lilac glow beneath, and judged the rising of the sun from this. Accustomed to the water, his breath came easily—though that year for some reason the water had penetrated his ears, clogging them, deafening him with a vast silence that under the sea was not unpleasant. Through

this vibrating silence the words of the legend repeated:
'Posa! Posa!' drumming with his strokes. And he saw
the carved-wood figure of the sea-Madonna painted blue
and rose and gold, weathered as with the paint of boats,
rising with the infant Christ in her arms, rising from the
still sea with feet trailed together in her long robe to form
the curve of a tail. The tube bobbing along on its cork
float gave him air, he gazed down only into a liquid
passing infinity—until suddenly, as it was almost possible
to imagine some storm-dragged wooden figure really
beneath him isolated in the water, a shape jagged and
flickering did indeed cut in underneath. He paused in
midstroke, startled. But it was only the beginning of the
rocks, the lowest arm of rock sliding suddenly into the
frame of his glass view like a dark unfocused insect under
the microscope.

He twisted away, he had swum farther in than he had
intended. No point in staying by the rocks at first; first
look for the possible tunny. He lay thus still, avoiding all
suspicious movement. Instantly almost, the clear water
focused and he saw the stony sea-bottom. Nothing moved.
Light as from an electric aquarium glowed from either
side. From such a light one felt how quickly the shadow
of a shape could move in. But nothing came. The stony
bottom, shingle and sand, stayed still, fossilized in the
water. Dead objects only—a sea-logged spar, some large
shells, the legless empty armour of a crab. So still it was
that Pietro saw at last a movement in miniscule that
normally could not have been noticed, a slight flickering
of feelers at the end of one whorled shell—a hermit crab
pouring out its soft body to pull the shell a laboured inch
along the floor.

So he lay there on his face, the unseen dawn rising
above, while the tide drifted him. It drifted him onshore

—so that just as in fact he was going to raise his head from the water, the rock-arm again obtruded itself swimming it seemed into the picture. This time it came not as a shadow but clearly, showing its thick growth of slowly moving weed. Pietro watched for a moment. He lowered one leg—the white movement might attract an octopus. But then abruptly he raised it, his body stiffened anxiously, something heavy had moved under the weed. His harpoon unbuckled, his finger on the trigger he waited, watching anxiously, back-paddling slightly against the drift so that he hung over that exact place. The weed remained closed. Then he saw, drifting out and disappearing again, like the end of a pointing finger, the tip of a pale tentacle.

His paddling hand went up to his mask. He knew the danger. Such an inch of tentacle was difficult to judge: it might belong to a small fish, it might be the tapering end of a full-sized arm. On that coast these creatures never grew to be giants, but the older parents weighed sometimes heavy enough to drag you down if they secured a firm enough grip on both the leg and a rock-arm on the floor. When that happened, it was no use hacking off the tentacle—another would writhe up in its place. Nor was it any good shooting, the tentacles would still hold. Only one tactic—an exercise that sounded fabuous told up in the air among the vines, but in the real water underneath was proved nevertheless the only recourse. It was to lift the mask—then dive down and bite the thing in the place between its two eyes, fastening the teeth and gripping. A nervous paralysis travelled the fat lengths of tentacle, the suckers retracted . . . but for the moment Pietro stayed alert. The octopus showed no sign of further movement.

The weeds remained closed. A thick black clustering

growth, about three feet off the rock, it extended on slender stems, and spread its rubbery fern above whatever lay below, hiding it completely: except when some exceptional current disturbed its slight, composed movement. But no current came, it remained only closed. So that now Pietro had to judge where the bulk of the fish should lie, calculating its position according to the rock's contour. Slowly he lowered his slender harpoon towards it, the long steel shaft tapered at what was hidden and about to be shot.

That word still echoed humming in his mind. 'Posa!' he muttered through clenched lips, and pulled the trigger. The shaft jolted down swiftly, almost vertically, at the weed.

The weeds fluttered as if a sudden hand had pulled at them from beneath; the harpoon sank into something and stopped, sticking up; but there was no lashing of a wounded fish, no monstrous outfly of tentacles. Pietro swore: he guessed he had missed; the thing must have crawled on, the harpoon stood now erected only in the thick weed. He began to pull in. The line tautened and held fast. He tugged. A slight give. The barb had caught in something firm, a rock crevice—now it was slipping away. And then the weeds parted, and pale flesh began to rise, slowly in the water, aerily as a heavy balloon. The flesh rose; as the weeds parted there grew from it a head and arms. But a head of streaming hair and two arms trailing outstretched, not tentacles, but fingered arms. Pietro stopped. Still the flesh rose, freed of the weed, emerging slowly until it became its full human body floating slowly up towards him hanging there on the surface—a body with streaming hair, a woman's body. Before he could recognize its features, he knew it was his wife.

(The house stood nearly above this rock projection, above tiers of vine terraces that rose from the landward end of the rockpoint. Perhaps in her sleep, perhaps consciously, she had decided to do away with herself and her pain; she had woken after he had left, risen, climbed down by the terraces, and here thrown herself into the receptive sea. Perhaps asleep, perhaps consciously at the end of her pain. . . .) His eyes swam watery; he heard the tragic music of the coast, of all this sea and ancient magic that sang still in the siren air, the great greek masks howling open their square mouths at the human misfall, the older tale of winds and surf and rock that stared impassively above the trifle of human striving. . . . Powerless he hung there, wanting to shudder away from this that floated up at him, seeing it now blurred through the watery film at his eyes, through the glassy mask, through the crystal water clear and still as air upon which it rose. Startlingly the image cleared. It was not his wife: it was a man.

That face was turned away. The harpoon had struck him in the side, up between the ribs. Now the shaft hung off to the side—like a soldier's spear. With a slow, sad motion, pleading in sorrow and baring a breast of agony, the two arms floated out to either side—in the water askew, but to Pietro's held eyes those arms were stretched wide on the cross. The head averted—dragged upwards by the harpoon, the body was trying to turn itself over face downwards—that averted head became the head of Christ. Abruptly in his shocked mind it was clear that here floating up towards him was Christ's body; extended in watery crucifixion; travelling upwards towards him; bearing thus a message; the son of the Virgin Mary of the Sea; the babe of the painted Madonna; the Madonna of the warning voice; the painted wooden

44

voice that had mixed with winds long ago to cry its Posa! Posa! . . . and as this body rose, the dawn above the surface widened, so that below water the purple glow brightened with a radiance of mounting music, a stained-glass hymn humming its windglass in his clogged ears.

Before the body touched him he jerked himself alive, threw the harpoon gun down at the sea-floor— quickly, quickly to get away, to act on this warning, to get out of the water, on to land and up to that house to prevent whatever might be happening. The body, lightly weighted by the falling harpoon, sank slowly away.

But this he saw only in a last instant. Already his head was up, the mask was off, and he was out above-surface in the full light of a red dawn. Glowing rose-red and reaching out immensely—on the islands, on the towering cliffs, on the near mountain-tops, on the aerial lines of straight cloud reaching away to the north, on the small domed town, on the sea now wild blue, there stretched this angry rose-red burning its colour across the vanishing greys and paleness. Pietro plunged fast through the water straight at a foothold in the rocks. His feet kicked up an unswimmerly surf, his arms flailed the water over-fast, he lost his breath and swallowed water. Coughing, he reached the foothold—it was quicker to get up by the terraces—and with water-blind eyes clambered up. Cutting his bare feet, he began up the rock, knowing blindly where the footholds lay, clutching and missing and gripping and sending down below a crumbling shower of small stone and earth. Then, at the first upward terrace, his eyes cleared, and to judge himself he looked back. A figure stood behind him, elevated against the sky on the jutting rock, on a rock-peak just above where he had fished, a figure precipitously poised on the very edge, her face lifted and gazing to sea.

The slight, cool wind still blew—it rippled the fine linen of her nightdress so that, in many light folds, it clung moulded against her body. An ancient garment thus in the dawn wind. She stood still, still as a figure erect can stand, with the ribbing of her shift moulded and stretched still, except where behind her small billows and ends fluttered. Her whiteness was warmed by the rose glow, but never so deeply as the red sky behind—that rumbling red sky-colour of the gods stretched an infinite back-cloth behind her; whitely too against the lichen-grey rock, the grave grey ancient rock upon which her naked feet were placed; whitely like a statue, face half turned to the sea. Then, suddenly his breath caught. He saw the markings on her face. Black smears round the eyes, red rough painting on the cheeks and ringing the mouth. Red and black pigments of a painted statue. Pagan-smeared rough colours, the soft æolian wind, the small fluttering like harp-music, the deep rose of a sky high in whose distant arc stretched clouds that hid the gods. Poseidon's daughter, the figure of classic immolation . . . and inextricably too the coast's Madonna. He crept up behind her, terrified to leave her free, fearing to wake her, and so with arms ready to clutch sang softly by her ear the slow notes of an old cradle-song.

The words whispered on to the wind, and very slowly, as if she heard from a great distance, she began to move, inclining her head, then turning, less it seemed of her own will than by some drawing power of the music itself. Then, carefully, he took her hand. He placed his face close to hers, so that she should not see what surrounded her. Her eyelids fluttered—suddenly opened wide, gazed

46

uncertainly, focusing his face . . . and then smiled. It was seconds later, past the time for shock, that she realized they were out on the headland.

Later that day, when he had got her to bed again, he went up to the carabiniere to report that dead body in the sea. By then his superstitions had receded, he realized its coincidence. The carabiniere telephoned through to neighbouring towns for news of a wreck, a drowning, a missing person—but without result. Finally, he put a message through to Naples, whose authority covered many miles of coast.

No news came within the week—it was plain that nobody all along that coast had been missed. They suggested that it might have been the body of a vagrant; or probably of a traveller unregistered. But no hotel or inn had missed a traveller. More curious still was the result of dragging operations at the foot of the cliff. No body was recovered. They found the harpoon exactly where it had been dropped. There was not a trace of flesh on the barbs. But then—the sea could have washed away such traces, or the fish nibbled them.

Curiously too—and of this Pietro thought one evening a week later as again he leant on his arched balcony and looked down from that stone house to the sea—curiously there had arisen on that day a fierce storm. The red dawn had been its herald, by midday the sun had disappeared behind racing grey clouds. The sea had sharpened with fierce Mediterranean waves, these small dark waves and their bristling white crests had coursed in endlessly throughout the day, smearing the beach with circles of foam, sending up a lash of spray by the wet black rocks. Such sudden storms have always an eerie quality after a stretch of so much undisturbed blue weather. They feel

47

like the direct result of wilful purpose. And the coming of
the rain was no less purposeful. Though Pietro had
watched several such visitations each year, the rain-gath-
ering on that particular day could be seen only through
eyes bemused by the morning's legend, felt to the beat
of a superstitious heart.

Rain clouds had gathered first far out on the horizon,
beyond the hump-backed siren islands, turning the sea
there deep purple—the purple of water overhung by
rocks. There, on the horizon, these clouds had first put
down their rain, vertically, so that one could see sharply
where the rain-shafts began, where they ended—as though
white pillars flanked some great bellying pantheon of
mist. The yellow sun had shone clearly to either side.
Then this broad temple of mist had begun to move—
shorewards. It came creeping over the water, growing
ever larger, shrouding the waves it crossed. It grew huge,
seemed to hover behind the whale-backed Sirenusæ, then
crept hungrily over them until their dark outline in turn
grew misted and finally disappeared. It came straight for
the land, and at one moment it was impossible from the
little beach to see the dwarf headland only some hundred
metres distant. Everything was hidden by the tall white
rain-mist, the edge of whose curtain one could see plainly
approaching across the near grey waves—and then it
seemed that a host of giant beings travelled within or
behind it, hidden and wishing it ruthlessly forward. The
mist so near seemed to leap. Abruptly the beach and the
township were enshrouded. A fine drizzle fell. And then,
thunderously under a house-high ceiling of cloud, came the
real rain. It fell sheeting, a downfall of water. In an
instant, as it touched, all projecting ledges and roof-
gullies poured water, thickly gushing cataracts of water.
The dried-up mountain stream rose like a wave and

washed a great semicircle of ochre mud over the beach. All gullies, all those rocky spouts of gargoyles tumbled down the brownish mud. The cliffs streamed with ledge-curtains. The sea, opaque green beneath the mist, took on an estuary's widening fan of mud. The vines bent, plaintains like broken blinds nestled closer to the earth. The domed roofs shimmered with leaden pellets. The whole stone town drooped like a wet pigeon; one minute of this waterous blow, and it seemed that the Tyrrhenian blue had never been. Out at sea, behind the mist and lighting it with ghostly radiances, the lightning spat its purple flicker. Thunder growled from the wide distance, the deep horizon.

It stopped quickly; withered, drizzled and was finished. The sun flared out. Fishermen swarmed from shelter like sparse hunting ants, hunting about their boats for damage, baling out the flood-water. A girl ran out with a copper pan and a bright lemon, squatted down, and began swiftly burnishing the pan with sand and the lemon. Life had again been allowed, somebody somewhere had been appeased.

Such a storm had meant more than its weird manner of arrival; it had meant the dragging of undercurrents at the body he had left down by the rock. And, surely enough, at the time of diving and dragging, it had gone. But even so—where? Seamen knew the currents and the intimate configuration of the coast, bodies will be washed only in certain directions, to places defined by the tides and currents, coves and inlets that yearly receive like hungry mouths their cold dessert. But this time they had gone hungry, no body had been washed up anywhere. According to all records, officially there had been no living body in the first place. Yet Pietro considered, frowning at the wide innocence of sea and sky, that most certainly he had

seen that body. Extended like the warning Christ to his
panicked imagination—but first, before that, though perhaps still in the same second, plainly he had seen it as a
drowned body. He could see again clearly its bloodless
pallor, its wish to turn; its sickening fishlike presence of
fat matter in the mineral water. The recollection was
vivid—but could he be sure it was not imposed afterwards
by a mind desperate for the practical solution? Could he
be certain that he ever saw anything—that it was not
some private vision, the edifice of previous foreboding
and those antecedent thoughts of the Madonna? And if
so, what constituted a private vision—did it come from
within, or was it imposed by unknown but always suspected forces from above?

He shrugged. There must have been a body. Everything, coincidentally, could be explained. A tourist arrived that day and not yet established in an hotel; drowning by some accident; and the body since impaled by the
storm on a sunken spar, some old iron anchor shaft out
on the sea bed. Easy. . . . But then he looked out at that
ancient sea, at the curious island group by which Odys-
seus strapped to the mast was rowed in his painted ship.
Once that ancient sailor had passed craving the magic
song, lulled by the deathly perfume of the narcissi which
fishermen in living memory had avoided with dreadful
instinct. Sea, sky, green vine and grey rock—calm and
innocent under sun. But immensely deep, one could not
see in this any cheerful bather's sea: it was too old,
steeped drunk with age. It held an omniscience of
life; no life of happiness and misery and the human
heartfelt struggle—but instead of earlier vitalities that
once preceded happiness and misery, acts of the gods,
the spilling of golden plenty and the thunderbolt of
punishment. A legendary sea—it was difficult not to

look round suddenly and think: 'Anything can happen here. . . .'

Suddenly, away on the beach, he noticed a movement. He stared, paralysed. A great black egg of rubber was moving up the beach, a monster jerking its way on cretinous legs across the lonely sand. He shuddered—then saw it was a boy, a summer visitor, carrying on his back an inflated rubber bathing raft.

THE BANK THAT BROKE THE
MAN AT MONTE CARLO

—

PIPER'S head ached with a smarting migraine, he had
drunk too much the night before. Moreover the mistral
blew hard, scudding grey round his brain. The bus shook
its tin plates as if one more turn of the Corniche would
shed them like unwanted metal wings ringing down on
to the hard road, when the rusted skeleton of the chassis
would still glide forward alone, digging its rods into
aching Piper. A loose window rattled glassily by his ear.
Voices argued to either side. A newspaper flicked his
right cheek, an elbow stuck into his constricted ribs.
Painfully he closed his eyes. They burned then against
the red lids; but at least with shut eyes there was no longer
the giddying steep coastline, no longer the recurrent
headlands cubed with bright villas, no longer the vista
of pine-sheltered bays each more rigorously beautiful than
the last, no longer the broad platitude of the sea to bear.
A glacier, a glacier to freeze this thunderous orange south!
A glacier alive with blood-drunk polar bears to guzzle
these lemon Latins! Polar bears . . . but ever dimly
against the flickering curtain of his closed lids Piper kept
thinking, irritably, of that little man from Nice whom he
knew to be sitting some seats behind. That pernicious
little man.

Two days before, he had been sitting in a deck-chair
on the promenade. Under the hot sun he and others
round him dozed or slept. He noticed that the man sitting
next to him sat also well back in his chair, at ease, as if in
fact dozing—but his eyes remained wide open. They

stared, round and lidless, into the full glare of the quivering hot-silver sea: one would have thought them glass eyes to withstand such direct heat. A private smile turned up the corners of his mouth.

They proved to be no glass eyes, but instead the eyes of a man on the watch, whose brain behind them wheeled without respite. Then a big-bosomed peaked-capped woman had placed herself between Piper and the sea—and this enormous black silhouette began talking rapidly in French. For a moment Piper could not understand—half-dozed, with ears unattuned to the strange fluent noise; but at last he realized that she wanted payment for his chair. Fumbling his French answer, he gave her the two francs. The woman passed on. But the man with the open eyes had been listening, and now instantly spoke, not moving, only turning his head and eyes, smiling only with his lips.

"You are Americain?"

"Eh?"

"Americain?"

"No, I'm English. . . ."

"Ah, English.'

He rolled the word over his tongue like a sliver of delicious veal. Then went on:

"I buy English pounds. Pounds sterling."

His lips stayed smiling, a loose lunatic smile, a dream of beautiful tastes: the eyes watched Piper sharply—but within themselves, somewhere behind the patina of scrutiny, played with private exquisitions, the copper-and-blue rustling of sweet pounds sterling.

"I'm sorry, I have no pounds, only a few. You know, we are not allowed much sterling; we carry money in the system of cheques, travellers' cheques."

"I buy travellers' cheques."

"No, you don't understand. These are no use to you, one signs them, cheques voyageurs."

"I buy them."

"But you can't cash them. They must be cashed personally, in front of a bank cashier."

"I buy them. How many have you?"

"Oh—some."

"I buy twenty, thirty, forty pounds. More."

"Sorry, I have none to sell."

"Ah—but you have pounds?"

"A few."

"I buy a few."

"Thank you—but no."

At this—into which Piper conveyed as graciously as he could a note of finality—a strange thing happened. For the stranger, instead of snapping off in some sort of surly displeasure, allowed instead the smile on his lips to grow large, and even his eyes to smile, as now he leant his neck back into the chair with a movement of most satisfied subsidence. Evidently he was as satisfied with the rejection of his offer as he had been by its proposal. As for Piper, he rose almost at once—allowing to elapse a polite minute of uneasy silence—and left the stranger still staring wide-eyed into the sun.

A few hours later, strolling along a street busy with shops glittering in the dusk and green trams looming larger against the approaching dark—Piper came face to face with the little man again. The eyes knew him instantly, the mouth curved again into a smile, assured and obsequious. A short babyish hand rose to the brim of his black felt hat, which then became elevated some inches exactly above the man's head. Piper smiled awkwardly, tried to pass—but the crowd was thick, the man stood straight in his path.

"Good evening. You are going to dinner? I tell you the finest restaurant in Nice. Fine food, good wine—you like wine?"

"Eh? Well—I like wine, but just now——"

"Go to Restaurant Grenoble, rue Berlioz. Finest in Nice."

"Well, thank you. Thank you very much. Now I must be——"

"But please—tell them I sent you. Tell them Robert sent you."

"Oh, thanks—yes——"

"Restaurant Grenoble. Robert. Good evening."

The man then sidestepped and mixed quickly into the crowd, worming in with his short body as though he were not of them, not of people, but instead some agile smaller being with a right to travel fast below eye-level. Piper moved on into a bar. He never visited the Grenoble, knowing it to be too expensive, and disliking the sense of ignorance, the itch of obligation that touting brings.

And now, this next day, in the mistral in the bus to Monte Carlo, here was the little man again. Piper resolved not to notice him. But a hangover, or any state of mental fatigue, brings with it not only brusqueness but also a tired tolerance: so that he knew he might fall easily now into this man's power. The best thing would be to slide away as quickly as possible, without talking.

The bus rattled past the Monaco brewery, cut round the cliff-side into the Place aux Armes. Perhaps there, in the little square of Monacoville, the man would descend? Piper watched from the corner of his eye through the window. Nobody descended. The bus continued down the street to the harbour and Monte Carlo's ascent. As they passed by a queer ravine decorated with a dwarf church, Monte Carlo came into near view. Piper's head jolted. The yellow extraordinary terraces broke over him with mad impact—this place could not be true! He felt as if small birds were pulling cotton strings from each side of his forehead, his head was expanding dangerously. As they drove beneath an immense ochre hotel inlaid with purple mosaics, as he saw beyond this surprising edifice something else called 'Balmoral,' and as the first sight of the sting-green cupolas of the birthday-cake Casino showed themselves—his mouth opened, and tasting the tobacco on his teeth, quietly he began to laugh. The laughing quivered in him like a further ache. The bus stopped exactly opposite the Casino doors by the ascending tropical garden, and still laughing painfully he navigated the aisle and descended. He was laughing blindly. He forgot all about the little man. He just stepped down into the full grey blast of the mistral and let it carry him, walking quickly up the pavement at the side of the gardens. The wind blew so strong, it was like a hand pushing. It bent the trees, made straight streamers of the hairy roots hanging from several more exotic branches, and up the crazy tilt of the hill Piper already saw four or five little boys almost leaving the ground, giving themselves to the wind's buffeting with excited cries that came and went in gusts of sound. The wind whirled the little boys round, flapping their coats up to their shoulders. Piper began to laugh loudly. Then above the wind heard himself—and made as fast as he could for the door of a bar. There, his head pounding, he ordered beer.

He remained standing by the bar, his eyes half-closed, looking straight down at the dull zinc counter. The barman fiddled low-down with a glass and the beer-tap. Until the glass was put before him, he kept his eyes down, fearful of meeting the barman's, fearful of conversation.

The room, small, was quite empty. Then the brassy beer was put before him, and the barman loitered off. Piper quickly drank half the beer. Its bubbles ran smoothly over his dry throat, his spine glowed with a muzzed comfort as if the spine itself drank. He raised his eyes. But there, in front of him, instead of the emptiness for which he had hoped, or perhaps an empty mirror with which he could play, stood a machine, an aluminium urn of great size that stood motionless and slightly steamed.

It stood on a shelf against the wall; it was itself four feet high, it towered above Piper. In that old-fashioned bar the urn's keen aluminium shone savagely, as though it were a visitor, an enemy visitor. From its implacable cylindrical body there stuck out a dreadful lacework of pipes—pipes winding downwards, upwards, sideways, turning corners at right angles, sweeping backwards in curves, or sometimes stopping abruptly capped in mid-air; all over these glinting pipes black knobs and taps were scattered—more of these than one could count; and on top of it all roosted a large aluminium eagle, wings outstretched. Piper shuddered. A cross between a squid and a Teutonic knight—fogged with stale alcohol such things appeared more than usually isolated, acutely static, static enough to move at any moment. A teutonic squid in silver armour that would at some moment soon begin to wave its arms at him—he shuddered again. Although it was of course no more than an urn, it was unbearable—and with all that steam it might blow up. Quickly he drank the rest of his beer, paid, and with a crash of the door was out again in the grey scudding wind.

Better a bit after the beer, he walked almost fast round the top of the sloping gardens. Then he stopped, bent by the wind, his coat collar flapping, his coat-tail letting sharp cold intrusions up his trouser-legs—and listened.

57

Not a sound above the whirring of the wind! And not a
person in sight! Not one person—from his present eminence he could see all down the avenue of the gardens to
the Casino and its terminal circus, all along a main shopping street to either side, all up a flight of steps to the
upper town—and not a living person: it was empty as a
dead man's town. Surely, he suddenly thought, that
pernicious little man at least would be about somewhere?
But no . . . not even he, no small scudding black-hatted
figure anywhere to be seen. The town was empty; the
Principality was empty for its short mile to either side—
of course because it was lunch-time, and at that the off-
season, and a day of mistral. Naturally no one would be
in the streets at this time, a quarter-past one o'clock.
How dead—Piper looked with longing for a few of the
earlier figures, the windblown little boys, two elderly
English residents, a scattering of Monégasque shoppers,
a solemn trooper of the Principality's guards in his
antique uniform of blue and red and white, a bus con-
ductor from France. But no one. Well, so it should be—
he would explore the lonely streets alone. And so he
began to walk very fast up and down dizzying flights of
steps, along fantastic streets, through the gardens, round
the Casino, and then up, up, up again to a high point
from which he could survey the whole. On this circuitous,
angled, dizzy perambulation he called in at several bars
for several drinks—beer, brandy, beer, brandy. Each of
the bars was equipped with a giant aluminium urn crested
with a shining eagle.

Half in memory, half seeing what he could see, Piper
tried to compress this odd Principality into some compre-
hensible form. In shape like what? A tolerant horseshoe?
A wide-horned moon, with on one horn the old citadel
jutting on its rock out to sea, with the sugar-cake Casino

primped on the other; in between—the harbour, with its
few winter yachts, its little light-houses, its miniature
gas-works; and in the belly of the moony horseshoe the
curve of Monaco and Monte Carlo converging, houses
and villas rising steeply up the bowl of small grey mountains that enclosed them. A doll's town, a devil's town, a
play-place for millionaires and a living place for Moné-
gasques. With what astounding ingredients, all set at
absurd angles along unmathematic streets. In an old
town set upon a hill the square-built houses grow easily
from the rock; but here the square-built villas jut off the
rock without growing, as if all those tiers of hotels and
erratic villas had been suddenly plaster-cast and at a
moment's notice lumped there—from which time they
stayed just stabilized by some effluence from the Casino,
the jingling power-house. Piper saw it under a sky grey
and fast-moving as a January sky in low-pressed London.
This grey now emphasized, as in the dark before a
thunderstorm, the bright colours and ornament of villas
meant for the sun.

In sunlight these tropicalities would have fused; but
now each one was seen to shine distinctly—yellow, pink,
white, green, purple villas; turquoise cupolas, jars of rose
faience, bright-grey sphinxes, cyclamen tiling on gas-
orange, peacock-blue shells opening to reveal no Venus
but pearl-grey pineapples. False corinthiana, false fes-
toonery, false balconies. One villa had walls set with
ultramarine tiling and gold arabic letters; another an
amber façade encrusted with paint-box-green flower-jars
and balconettes, turrets, canopies. In between this conglomerate of giddy shape the streets rose and fell at
inaccurate levels, while from tier to tier hundreds of steps
fell at steep, intensely accurate drops. One poster invited
a visit to the Café Betty Smith, where César et ses Boys

would entertain. Another defied that one should miss
'*La Danse Atomique*, TA-MA-RA-BOUM-DI-HE.' All roads
led to the Casino, to gardens of giant cactus knobbly with
red pears, to descending lawns of emerald needle-high
grass, to gardens where roots hung from the branches of
trees and each flower seemed freshly polished and waxed
by its private gardener—and to the astounding Casino
itself, an intricate fin-de-siècle factory of sugar-icing plaster, violet-glass lamps, verdigris roofs. In front of this
now stood again a long white bus and a spiked, helmeted,
blue-red-and-white Monégasque guard: Piper descended
the gardens, his head grey with the horizontal wind,
dazzled. From the doors of the Casino there emerged a
little man in a black hat.

Monsieur Robert saw Piper immediately—possibly he
had remained there at this central point all the time—and
seemed now literally to be blown towards him, his hat
raised again exactly above his head. Piper allowed himself to be blown backwards into the doorway of a bar—
but before the door closed the little man was in too.
Together they turned to the bar, sat down opposite an
aluminium urn, and above two glasses of brassy beer
gaped upwards at the silver eagle. It was only a quarter
to two. Piper's whole walk had taken no more than half
an hour. It seemed much longer. He was not drunk. But
the hang-over had lengthened time for him, isolating each
perception, magnifying the presence of objects met and
the moments clinging round them. Now he felt cornered.
The little man said:

"You have tea, coffee, cocoa?"

"No."

"English tea?"

"No, I have not."

"You bring sugar with you—coffee?"

"I have brought nothing with me, no tea, coffee, cocoa, sugar, nothing, nothing, nothing."

"No cocoa?"

"No."

"Aaaah!"

Once again the little man's smile grew larger with defeat, he seemed to swell with satisfaction, to drink his beer with such a slow pleasure that it might have been cocoa, tea, coffee and sugar all together. He smiled at the eagle as though he might kiss it. Suddenly he said, looking sharply at Piper's left hand:

"What is time?"

"Time? I don't know. . . . Oh yes, two o'clock."

"You have no watch?"

"No."

"No watch on the wrist?"

"No."

"Ah, you have a watch in the pocket!"

"I—have—no—WATCH."

"Watch on the waistcoat, perhaps?"

Since Piper then frowned hard and impatiently at him, the man Robert was forced to see that Piper had indeed no watch, and for a moment his smile faded and he shook sadly his black-hatted head. Then his loving smile crept back, and with infinite tenderness he exposed his own left wrist, upon which was gold-strapped a flat gold watch. This he smoothed lovingly with his short fingers.

"I like to have a watch. Here is the best you can buy. Swiss watch. This watch tells always the right time. See— ten to two hours."

"Well."

"I always have watch."

"I'm sure."

"But I sell it. I sell it now for ten pounds."

"Not to me you won't."

"Twelve thousand francs."

"I don't want a watch."

"I sell—you don' want a *watch*?"

"The answer is in the negative."

"Please?"

"No. Certes. En point NON."

"Ha, ha! He jokes. He say he don' want a *watch*. Eleven thousands francs three hundreds. Nine pounds."

"Good bloody bye."

And not before seeing the little man's smile begin to spread again over his wet lips, Piper was up and crashing again out of the door into the mistral. The wind held him for a moment—a moment too long. Robert was there at his side, hat raised a vertical inch.

"Please, the patron say you have forgot pay for the beer. Twenty francs, please. I pay for you?"

Piper was going to ask why the hell he hadn't paid himself—when suddenly he crumpled inside, exhausted, and fumbled in his wallet for a note. Then he paused, noting the way Robert's face seemed to peer closer at the money, as if he were going to eat it—and turned back into the bar. At this Robert again raised his hat and was off. Inside, the barman asked him for fourteen francs.

Well, he thought, Robert is above all consistent. Tourists behaved so brashly they deserved such persecution. The making of money was a reasonable pursuit. Piper's own predicament was at that time grave—it was the cause of his drinking so heavily the night before. He had very nearly exhausted his money. It had seemed pointless to worry about the few thousands francs left—so he had drunk most of them up. He still had his ticket back to England. But England was blank, England now held nothing for him, no home, no job, no money, no

62

wife. Certainly he might perhaps obtain another job, another wife, some more money, even a home; but he felt no drive towards these substitutes, they felt far away— the material distance had its effect—they felt pointless. To forget his troubles he had come south. Now he had arrived at the end of a period of anæsthesia. To-morrow he would have to make a decision. But that would not be so if he had money. Money could postpone indefinitely. The sorrow it would never cure: but as a palliative, a pro-crastinator!

Money, thought Piper. And he looked far round and along the intersecting roads for a sign of Robert. He was nowhere to be seen. The only course was to search the streets again—and so this Piper set out to do, turning into the wind again, walking fast.

After what seemed an hour—but was probably twenty minutes—of angling round corners and up and down those inclines and staring in above the curtains of bars, he found himself on the sloping esplanade that led down to the harbour. Monaco on its rock towered opposite, the ancient citadel facing out to sea. So down the esplanade skidded Piper, through the orange-trees lining the short streets of the harbour quarter, and then up slowly the steep stone gradient zigzagging across that precipitous rock face to the citadel town above. The white embattle-mented towers of the Prince's Palace stood out like snow against the grey sky. Piper climbed higher, passing great iron rings set in the fortress walls, entered beneath grim arches—and finally emerged on to the parade square in front of the Palace. At this eminence the wind blew fiercer than ever, roaring flatly across the square, pulling with it the supple branches of a young tree so that they streamed like hair in a current, battening the cloaked sentries into their red-and-white-striped sentry-boxes, only leaving unmoved the line of long cannon trained out over the seaward ramparts.

He crossed over the square and entered a maze of narrow, huddled streets. Here there was shelter from the wind, but the streets were silent, empty. Stout wooden doors stood shut, as if at a time of plague. Yet the mellowness of these old streets quietened his mood, here was a sort of impersonal sanctuary, still, venerable. How more emphatic the shock then to debouch from such quietude on to a sudden space bounded by one of the largest buildings he had ever seen in his life, a giant edifice of white stone, pillared, friezed, top-heavy, a monstrous, false, classic pile out of all proportion to that miniature citadel, and built exactly on the edge of a sheer rock drop some hundreds of feet flat on to the sea. The Oceanographical Museum!

And on the wide white steps there stood a little man in a black hat.

"Robert! Monsieur Robert!" Piper cried, giddied by the shock of this monstrous edifice, running towards the little man.

He could not have heard, for there were fifty yards of wind flying between them—but nevertheless he turned, saw Piper, and instantly fled away up the steps. Like a black-hatted fly he vanished through the immense glass doors. Piper chased after him. But already Robert was past the ticket-bar, and Piper was blocked both by an official and what might have been a provincial gentleman and his wife. This man's wife chattered shrilly, while unperturbed her square-faced husband searched his pockets. At last he found what he sought, a crumpled old season ticket, and passed through the barrier. Even then, still blocking the barrier, with Piper dancing his agitation behind, he loitered as his wife pointed up at a giant deep-sea fishing net that hung like a brown spider's web from the giddily high ceiling.

"Qu'est-ce que c'est que ça? Ça! Qu'est-ce que?. . ."

The man measured it coolly with his eye, with some distaste, and shrugged his shoulders.

"C'est un filet."

At last Piper was round them and running up the steps into the museum rooms. He stopped abruptly before the red plaster dummy, lifesize, of a Japanese landcrab, a creature like a murderous table poised on tall feathered legs as high as his waist, and under which he saw written with academic relish: '. . . ils aiment surtout le chair humain.' Abruptly he came to his senses.

He had come to a stop somewhere near the centre of a long hall filled with glass cases. These housed a thousand different creatures of the sea—from a narwhal to a seaslug, a giant swordfish to a pale, sunless prawn. Case upon case of glassy ice enclosing their frozen suspended seafruit; and obtruding among and above them rose large plaster representations and the colossal bones of whales. All whales, Piper saw mazedly, wore giant beards, through which giant draughts of sea-water were out-filtered, so that the solid little seafoods were retained inside as against a hairy strainer; and now, looking at one such mass of coarse brown beard, he noticed above it, as if also retained, something small and black, dented and brimmed. He brought his eyes to focus—far over the room, a little black hat, Monsieur Robert! As nearly as possible he ran towards him. In and out of the cases, past all those glassy fish he ran; and drew near to Robert gazing with wide-thinking eyes at the fœtus of a baby whale, a thing of cooked sweetbreads dragging its umbilical from a caul of crushed cellophane. But really the eyes of that Robert concentrated on some other matter of the mind—and now as Piper approached this alert organ warned him, he turned, saw Piper, and made off quickly, dodging among the cases, bending his knees to lower his height.

Piper followed as fast as he dared. In that vast echoing place where people talked in whispers, neither really could run—but instead walked very fast. Not as racers walk, with hands clenched and chests out, but as shadows walk, with long gliding steps. Out of the first hall they went, into the vestibule, up an enormous stairway; past pale water-colours of Spitzbergen into a further hall, this one filled with trophies from the arctic. Past a wax eskimo in his kayak, past penguins and ambergris, shells and fossils and curious nets, past brass-bound instruments for measuring the depths, past wicked harpoons and cases of salt—until suddenly, somewhere among the halls, the vestibules, the stairways, Monsieur Robert disappeared.

Absolutely. As if he had passed through the wall itself. Piper stopped, his head aching as much from the impact of so many weird objects—things that in their very death seemed more fixedly alive, with greater presence and a strange still power—as it ached from alcohol-crying blood; and stared about him in the cold, clear light that was shed everywhere from those tall museum windows. His heart pumped, his tongue and teeth felt hot and yellow, his mind anticipated some immense cracking shot-sound that would split it into instant madness. Then he saw, in a small niche in the wall, a narrow door marked: 'Aquarium, Ascenseur.'

He loped forward and rang the bell. The lift attendant asked for two francs, and then they were descending down for what seemed hundreds of feet into the rock itself. At last the lift stopped, the door opened, and Piper entered the polished dimly lit oceanographical aquarium. It was so dark that for some seconds he was unable to make out

66

the features of the slow-moving human silhouettes that passed in front of the slow-moving fish in their illuminated tanks. He looked harder—but no sign of Monsieur Robert. However, the way was clearly marked—one had to follow a certain direction bounded by brass rails—so Piper started, dodging as he could past whom he could. Past now upright red hermit crabs like old women in bonnets, past old women in bonnets; past smart black and scarlet prawns, past dowdy provincial observers; past a huge old turtle waving its flappers in a submarine motion of slow flight, past an old man dribbling water from his mouth; past a large hollow stone from whose many holes stared the agonized faces of eels, helpless with laughter—and past other faces that looked as though they had never laughed; past—but here Piper was stopped: there was a small steadfast group in front of this tank, a tank containing a small octopus.

He recognized again the provincial gentleman and his wife who had first blocked his entrance at the ticket bureau. Now these two loitered in front of the octopus. The octopus swam slowly from side to side in his illuminated water. Tentacles like films of soft soap weaved about the eyed head, the disgusting lizardly pouch. On the sandy floor beneath lay the bones of very small crabs. With the acute lateral movement of an indonesian dancer, the octopus's head moved from side to side as if wishing to get a better look at the provincials, who themselves stared the harder. The woman was horrified—she almost sobbed, prodding her husband in the ribs:

"Qu'est-ce que c'est que ça? Ça! Qu'est-ce que?. . ."

To which the old man answered, with a shrug of his shoulders and the same look of cold distaste:

"C'est un poulpe."

But these loiterers proved in fact to form a kind of

cover for Piper, because as now they moved slowly on they hid him from the next dark human shape peering into the next tank—they circumvented this figure, and Piper was standing an inch from Monsieur Robert's shoulder. Monsieur Robert was staring with his wide eyes into the tank, in which swam also a wide-eyed thoughtful fish. For a moment the most perplexing creature of all, lurking in a dark unlit tank. But it was no fish—only Monsieur Robert's face itself, now joined by Piper's face, the two reflected in the dark polished wall where a tank might have been. As with second sight the unseeing eyes of little Robert now caught sight of the second face by his own, he turned sharply, saw Piper, and knew that this time there was no escape. In that instant Piper gripped his arm. Monsieur Robert began to speak quickly, whining up like a dynamo:

"Ah, it is you. Now I must make my excuses, I am most sorry, it was all a mistake, the patron first has said these drinks are costing twenty francs——"

But Piper stopped him:

"Forget it, forget it. Monsieur Robert—would you like to buy some English pounds?"

Now for the first time Monsieur Robert looked sad. It was plain that of all matters in the world, English pounds sterling interested him the least. One could not tell, for instance, whether the present exchange rates would remain firm. He himself suspected that England was not so secure as was generally believed. Who could tell? It was a great risk. However—how many pounds had the Englishman got?

So up in the lift they went, out through the great glass museum doors, out into the wind again and on to a quiet corner of a terrace overlooking the harbour. There, by a large pile of rusting cannon-balls, Monsieur Robert bought Piper's remaining six pounds at the rate of 750 francs the pound—100 francs less than the rate he had offered the day before. However, from his wallet he produced a brand-new note for 5,000 francs and handed this to Piper—and this was enough for Piper's purpose. There in the wind the transaction took place, as all over the coast similar exchanges were being made—and the wind fluttered the notes and the coat-tails of the two figures standing bowed with their heads close together, somehow managing to talk in whispers yet above the wind. Finally they shook hands, the little man walked off in one direction, and Piper stumbled away to the downward harbour path. From such a high point one could see straight across the harbour, across the Principality itself: over the few bobbing yachts, the terraces, to where the white casino stood, glittering its towers and green roofs against the grey sky.

The Casino doors admitted him from the wind; inside, it was warm and polished, quiet and elegant and smooth. With some odd change he paid for his entrance, then exchanged the whole 5,000 francs for counters. He entered the halls of play. It was the afternoon, few people were about. He approached one of the tables: a table of whispers among the soft insulations of carpet, beneath high domed ceilings, between gilded brown walls. It was like a terminal hall, a terminal for the final, infernal funicular. There was the soundless smell of green cloth. He placed all his counters on one number.

While the ball swung its excited ellipse over the frets he waited, nervous and tired. He had intended to use this last few thousands francs carefully, to play with a cunning economy. But in such sudden massive quiet he lost his will; he had not had a drink for more than an hour; such a sudden withdrawal of the wind left him deflated.

In any case, it could scarcely matter whether he won or lost in the end. But he won. He was in a moment the owner of counters worth 175,000 francs.

His energies mounted. He gathered up the counters and made for the bar. There, while the magic discs weighed his pocket, the barman mixed him a very large brandy and iced seltzer; it cooled and fired his body, he congratulated himself on his good fortune, on the prospect now of many further idle weeks in the South, and particularly on such a triumph over Robert. How irritated he would be to know! How cheated! Piper almost left his seat in order to find Robert at once and tell him—and then he stopped himself. This new power had filled him with a sense of cunning. Avoid Robert at all costs—he would only have to buy a watch. Instead—perhaps a further stake at the tables?

He finished his brandy and walked slowly across into the whispering quiet hall. This time—he winked to himself—he would play carefully; indeed, now there was no reason for precipitate decisions, the hours lay ahead at leisure. He selected counters worth five thousand francs, and placed it on the even numbers. He lost.

Perfectly at leisure, he waited. He let the wheel turn. Then he placed a further five thousand francs on the even numbers. He won. He smiled to himself—so the wheel, the croupiers, the whispering watchers thought he was 'caught'? No, not this time. He had no intention of letting his new-won leisure drift away, this leisure that was his breakwater against disaster. He pocketed his counters and turned away towards the door.

A man wearing a white tie, a grey-haired smooth man who had been whispering to one of the croupiers, now hurried over and spoke quietly in Piper's ear. Would the gentleman be so kind as to accompany him to the office—

a little matter. . . . Piper replied that he would be delighted; in fact, that was his immediate destination. The man with the white tie bowed his head and nodded a long-drawn, appreciative 'Aaah!'

For some reason the office door was closed quietly, efficiently and finally behind them. Officials rose to their feet.

"This is the gentleman?"

"This is he."

"Without doubt."

"Then we must endeavour to arrange the matter as quickly, as quietly, as discreetly as possible. Sir—I must ask you to return to this office the counters in your possession. To the value of one hundred and seventy-five thousand francs."

"But that is exactly what I came here for—to return them. . . Here they are——"

"Ah!"

"Good."

"The gentleman finally has the good sense——"

"What do you mean, the good sense?"

"Perhaps—to know when he has lost?"

"Lost? What are you talking about?"

"Ah!"

"Well, if it amuses you—and now, my francs, one hundred and seventy-five thousand."

"Your francs?"

"Please, gentlemen. Enough. One hundred and seventy-five thousand francs in exchange for the counters here——"

"Sir, this is no time to joke. We have tried to be discreet in this matter——"

"Then I wish to God you'd be indiscreet. And please be quick. One hundred and seventy-five thousand francs."

"You know very well you have no francs————"

"What!"

"I beg of you, quieter. It is better not to create a scene————"

"Scene? Will you please hand me my money?"

"You mean————?"

"One hundred and seventy-five thousand francs I mean."

"You mean—you don't understand?"

"Understand what? What? WHAT?"

"That your note was false—counterfeit?"

As this was said, and as with a gradual declension of his whole inside Piper realized the meaning of those men's pronouncements, the three or four faces in front of him seemed to lose their surety, to grow dismal, as though envisaging each such a future as faced Piper. In fact, they had all in a second realized that after all Piper was in ignorance of the quality of his note; that what had seemed a simple settlement would now become a long and intricate argument, lasting perhaps for hours; that belief, unbelief, accusation, recrimination would follow their interminable course; that legal aspects would arise, perplexities compound upon themselves—as to a retention of the winnings if the first five thousand were made good, as to the bona fides of the gentleman if the previous handler of the note confessed, and so forth and so forth. Throughout the afternoon.

And so it was to be. Piper's head was greyly swelling, the room seemed all glass and faces, the sensation of being in a foreign land grew acute, old national distrusts rose and wheeled about his mouth, those three or four officials at times turned into five or six, their dark faces all spoke at once, their lips dragged downwards and their eyebrows rose inwards in tiers of deprecatory 'U's', talking hands fluttered on all sides, exasperation seemed to veil darkly the light, and all the time the hope within him sunk lower and lower through his stomach. As the strength left him, the guilt grew and a sense of condemnation with it. But this did not take all the afternoon. It took no more than ten minutes. By which time Piper, knowing what odds he faced, had relinquished all claim to the winnings, while the officials agreed to believe him innocent of an attempt to pass a false note. And thus he left the office, passed out through the polished doors and, again caught in the wind, walked blindly round the Casino to the terrace behind it overlooking the sea.

There he stood, leaning against the inward-blowing wind, and alone realized, more deeply, with ever-growing intensity, his situation. No wife, no money, no job, no home—a thousand miles from his no-home. A quarter of an hour before he had possessed a key to forgetfulness. His hands deep in his coat pockets touched a wallet. He drew this out, and sheltering it in his coat against the wind, saw the green paper of his return ticket. He snatched it, stretched his arm at full length above his head as though he were flying a kite, let the ticket flutter in the wind, then opened his fingers. It went sailing high on the wind like a sudden green bird, darted to vanish up among the trees of the gardens behind. An access of martyrdom like a physical secretion rose in Piper's empty frame—he drew out the last note, the final fifty francs, and caused his arm to raise it high. But as the money crossed his eyes, he lowered his arm and replaced the note carefully in the wallet. His throat felt dry.

Just then he turned and caught sight of the Casino building, its rear façade. A laugh coughed from his wind-dried lips. So it was here, beneath this absurd façade, on these immaculate tea-time terraces, that so many of the distraught had blown away their brains! This, the terrace of suicide! Beneath the twisted sugar-plaster, the wild mosaic, the insoluble rich bric-à-brac of the Pleasure-drome! On these terraces, red-sanded and swept to a Dutch perfection, regimented with flowers and dotted with seats painted red and silver, the neatest and nicest place in the world! Why—before the revolver was out of one's pocket, a gardener would already be there with his enamelled white basin to trap the first drop of blood, and after him other gardeners, with fresh sand.

But the laugh left him, there entered his muddled brain a perilous: 'Why not?' Words that have occasioned so many of the extreme deeds, deeds of high valour, relapses of withering failure; words that shrug their shoulders of proportion and perspective, accounting for no more than the moment. In Piper's shocked brain the words grew big, and he entered into that state of which coroners say: '. . . The balance of his mind was disturbed.' Unbalanced, but extraordinarily cunning, keenly balanced indeed as far as the purpose was concerned. He looked up quickly at the Casino—no, not there. Besides, he had no gun. He looked at the terrace balustrade, and saw beyond it the towering citadel. Monaco! The Museum! He ran round the Casino, and saw there waiting the long white surgical bus. He boarded it. Soon, again with windows rattling in his ears, he was whirling again down the esplanade and away from Monte Carlo. But not on the return journey to Nice, this time up the rock to the dizzy Musée Océanographique.

The tall glass doors were still open, the same attendant handed him his ticket, the same massive halls received him. Some of the same people seemed still to be wandering among the cases. They belonged to a time, only a half-hour previously, when decisions had been taken by the world against him: now, elated in his singularity of purpose, he praised himself that the decision was now his and his alone uniquely against the world. And he was now almost running again, gliding swiftly towards his objective.

This lay in what seemed to be a jutting bay of the building, jutting from the rock and overhanging the sea itself. There, in the centre of a vacant space of floor, was erected a small circular balustrade of stone, as high as a man's waist. It enclosed no fish-pool, no rare exhibit— but instead a hole. A good-sized circular shaft through whose lower end one could see vertically down to the sea a hundred vertiginous feet below. White little waves in miniature played on the rocks at canyon depth. It was like peering over the side of an aeroplane and seeing far beneath one the doll-like seascape. One stood on firm ground and felt revolted by the cruel, straight, endless drop.

Piper gripped the stone of the balustrade, and with a smile of triumph at the few people scattered round, a smile as conscious as a suicide's letter, he leaned over, drank in the vertigo, let this draw his head and threw himself toppling into the eye of the abyss.

He landed painfully sprawled a few feet below—on a thick platform of polished glass. One foot was bent under his thigh, and now burned with hot pain. For some seconds the shock had him stunned. Then he awoke to his situation—to a broken ankle, a glass platform at the base of a smooth cylinder of stone, and to this final and ludicrous reversal of his great personal decision. He broke out laughing in good earnest.

Minutes later, still laughing, he looked up to see several heads peering above him over the balustrade. There again was the provincial man and his wife. As from a great distance he heard her voice, shrill, repeating in hennish fixation:

"Qu'est-ce que c'est que ça? Ça! Qu'est-ce que c'est? . . ."

But at last the cold distaste of the man was warmed, he raised now both his eyebrows and peered closer:

"Ah, ça c'est un humain. . . ."

TUTTI FRUTTI

"ME? Oh, I'm a *fatalist*. . . ." The mind shrieks, longs to take by the ear that self-congratulatory breed of martyrs and scream once more the high litany of 'fate,' verse by verse—the scheme of cycle and coincidence, antipathies of freewill and of the mind enslaved, the effluence of the wish, fear and its invitation to disaster, the quest for euphoria, probabilities of accident and the certainty of chance.

However—it was not so easy to condemn the last man who drove at me these famous words. His circumstances were too awful, he had been punished enough. This man —Ohlsson—had suffered most severely at the hands of what he called 'Fate.' But to the beginning . . . with Ohlsson some years before limping from the railway station into the sunshine of a southern city, Nice.

Limping from the long-constricted journey with its aching night, its stenches of intimacy; from the lavatory wash in stale trickling water; from the corridor's litter of paper and peelings and leaning bodies; limping, at a remove, from the year spent in the north, in a town of smoke and railways, of brass and soot; limping—but now coming out into the full glare of the flat blue sky, seeing sun-yellow buildings and the high tufted palms, seeing fringed silk curtains and sunblinds and jalousies and white umbrellas and all other cloth filters for the sun— as from alcohol his back shivered with sudden warmth. He hailed a taxi as though he were hailing the whole South. And thus warming, sat back as this softly cushioned motor drove him swaying down the boulevards—

straight, leaf-shaded, with shop-windows glinting darkly in the night of high noon—to the main square and his hotel.

There, with mounting expectation, he followed the processes of arrival—pleasurably painful processes, like the sweet ache of unfreezing. The lassitude of unpacking; the complete wash, stripping the skin of rough travel, emerging with a pale feeling; for half an hour an imposed rest on the new bed—when the mind refused to sleep, wheeling and gathering its momentum of impatience, hot as the sunlight darkening through the shutters. At last the hands of the clock crept to the end of that half-hour. Ohlsson was off the bed with some sort of a jump, marvellously refreshed, whistling, allowing himself the luxury of a few words aloud to himself. And then, feeling the clean linen of a fresh shirt, he was flinging open the double shutters and receiving to himself this new city of his arrival.

There lay the fine wide Place Masséna. On one side a garden of palms led to the milk-blue sea. But elsewhere rose a warm geometry of classic, arcaded buildings washed in pinks from pale rose to dark terra-cotta; hundreds of rectangular shutters were picked out in green, in a succession of greens, olive to lizardly yellow. No blues, no oranges here—but instead the colours of the moss-rose, rose and olive, with the pale pavements between and only high above the blue of sky, so brilliant that it had ceased to be domed, flat, hot and immense. Ornamental lamps islanded the broad square; in the centre stood a line of black carriages, red-wheeled and polished, with fine leathern canopies and white-capped horses.

To Ohlsson, who was on an errand of romance, who expected of this holiday some sort of an adult fairy tale, and who had in fact sufficient hope to be capable of

78

obtaining this—the vista of such a square proved perfect.
His pleasure rose, he knew with certainty that everything
was now promised. And a few minutes later he was down
walking through the arcades and marvelling that the
ceilings still revealed a faded painting of roses and rib-
bons, of putti and florid friezes, of mandolins and exotic
fruits; and that pillars beneath painted corinthian capitals
still showed a leprous residue of curled lettering advertising from another century: "CHOCOLAT KLAUS"; "BANQUE
DES VALEURS METALLURGIQUES"; "LE PARFUM DE LA
VRAIE VIOLETTE"; and even a performance at the Opera
dated some seventy years before. Everywhere hung the
faded fragrance of expansive years that had offered all the
fruits—the chocolate-box years. Years of parasol and
cylindre, of Verdi and Berlioz and Paganini, of patchouli
and the attars. Here were the streets themselves: Rue
Verdi, Rue Berlioz, Rue Paganini, Rue Buffa! And the
carriages themselves as fresh as new—many of them, no
solitary relics! And the curled railings, the iron lamps,
the small iron-works everywhere not derelict but in as
full use still as the fringed silk blinds in the railway office,
as the red and silver plush canopy of a merry-go-round in
the Place Garibaldi, as the wrought-iron pergolas, as the
mosaics of yellow villas, as the balconies and the wide
squares with their dusty trees, squares so spacious and
beaten flat by years of the changeless, flowery sun.

Ohlsson wandered about, tasting the sweet-sour. In
such a mood, one sees only what one wants to see, selects
from the conglomerate only those facets that reflect the
exact desire. Much else goes unseen. A false chiaroscuro
takes the mind—Ohlsson's light now shone on the many
living remnants, while the shade obscured modernistic
cinemas, bars of false Burgundian darkness, political
streamers, the emptiness of the cafés, and over all the

misery of an inflated cost of living. When for a moment
he grew conscious of these matters of the shade, wearily
in a weary world he suspected that once again, if the truth
should be sought, he must bring himself to enter into the
present life of the people—and if he could not help, then
at least shake his head with their suffering, observe a
succession of two-minute silences in their sympathy, sober
his gay mood to tune with their low-strung discord. But
was this obligatory, always? Was no respite allowed?
Ohlsson stood for a moment irresolute, the lightness
shading. Then he sighed, shrugged, smiled up again at
the flower-frescoes on the arcade ceiling and turned into
a restaurant for lunch. He was on holiday. He lunched
off a well-oiled salad, grilled sardines freshly fished,
roasted chicken from Bresse, aubergines, cheese, grapes,
a persimmon, good red wine.

Fortified, this tall ash-haired Swede stepped once
more into the sunshine of the square, prepared now for
further pleasure, for adventure. And this he was soon to
find—his faith put him in charge of events. At other
times, indeterminate and doubtful, he would have seen
too clearly the whole perspective, he would have found
this too distressing to accept his joy without shame, he
would have worked no magic on events. But not just then.

Across the square again, past the delicate clustered
lanterns and towards the sea. The palm garden lay in
between—each tree with the acute independence of palms
defined separately against the blue beyond, a tall sprouting
of feathers clutched high on each pachyderm pole.
Ohlsson received them with joy. It was November, the
reality of palms was magic. He paused for a moment,
absorbing the exotic pattern. From behind him came a
neat clopping of hooves, a music of harness. He turned to
see a carrozza approaching. Alone on the carriage-way,

elegant, its whole equipage swaying with animal grace. He hailed it.

As the driver reined his horse, and as Ohlsson had opened his mouth to give his direction—another voice spoke from the opposite side of the carriage, a woman's breathless high arpeggio. The carriage-driver turned his head from Ohlsson to the woman, who was hidden behind the horse's rump; then, as Ohlsson also spoke, turned back to him. Then back to the woman, then to Ohlsson— perched up on his box and switching his head like the spectator of a ball game. His leathery old face smiled, his shoulders shrugged—and he lapsed back to wait. Ohlsson was saying: "I want to take a long drive round the town. . . ." At the same time the woman moved into view and said: ". . . to make a tour for the afternoon. . . ."

They both smiled. It was the day for it. Soon they were seated side by side inside the shell-like awning.

Just as the driver cracked his whip, for that short second, Ohlsson saw something which seemed to finalize like a rising cymbal-rich chord this overture to his luck. His head was turned towards the lady when suddenly, in a moment that he was to remember for a very long time, he saw the cut of her profile outlined against a wall of most curious pale turquoise beyond. Framed by the dark carriage hood, her ear-rings flashed gold, brilliant points of yellow lit dark olive eyes, her white teeth smiled luminously, a fine shadow of moustache softened the course of deep vermilion lips; the lace frill of her dress surfed white in the sun; and all this cut a strange and lovely picture against the curious turquoise wall beyond. He peered to see what such a wall could be. As they moved off, he saw—it was the wall of a pagoda, a wall of turquoise faience inscribed with birds of paradise and floating cherry blossom, and held together in a pale-

brown framework of cast-iron bamboo. With delight he
saw this edifice to be a supreme gift to him from the past,
more than ever Flora Dora, the epitome of tutti frutti.
It was a pissoir. Then they were off.

Throughout the afternoon's heat they drove along the
plane-flecked boulevards, along avenues of ochre mansions frogged with pale-grey shutters, past palms fat as
pineapples and stoned gardens of blue cactus. Cafés under
their broad awnings slept empty, their broad doorways
dark in the midi torpor. Along the Promenade des An-
glais they drove, admiring the portentous glare of sugar-
white hotels curving round the sea. Soon Ohlsson's pale-
haired hand touched hers: those other brown fingers did
not draw away.

They stopped at the flower market. He bought her
two sorts of red carnation—vermilion and crimson—and
the coral friction of two such reds glinted like a beautiful
poison against her brown skin and her dress of white lace.
She thanked him, first smiling her eyes directly into his,
then turning her face away with an admirable coquetry.
She did nothing so that more should be done. And a little
while later, in the carrozza trotting along the edge of the
sea, past a line of African palms, past the white terraces
of the hotels, and above the hotels the purple mountains
hazed in the heat that formed such a warm protective
curtain round this wide Bay of Angels—Ohlsson drew
that woman back into the shadow of the canopy and
slowly, unresisted, sank into her lips. She shuddered, and
still with closed eyes turned away her head; but gripped
his arm closer.

At tea, in a room of high glass windows framed in royal
white, in such a cool room overlooking a lawn of cropped
English grass and red tropical flowers—he told her he

was on holiday, and that this was his first day. She told him of a year's seclusion—a result of widowhood—and that this was only her second week again in the sun. The time came when Ohlsson judged his moment to press further. He invited her to dine that evening.

"But I have already shared your carriage and taken your tea!"

"You know it was a pleasure—please——"

"Then——"

"Please."

"Then I agree. But it must be my dinner. I shall expect you at eight o'clock."

"But, I could not——"

"At eight?"

A pause. Then Ohlsson said:

"Then I must agree. . . . I'd better know your hotel?"

"Villa. Called de Bordighera, in the Rue Buffa. At eight—but I must ask you a favour——"

"Anything."

"You will come at eight. But this will be for an aperitif only. I am alone, you see, with only one maid—I can scarcely expect her to provide a reasonable dinner on such short notice. But when she has left, later on, at about ten, I can get us supper——"

It is easy to imagine with what feelings Ohlsson returned to his hotel. But such good fortune is suspect. After his first elation he considered the matter more carefully. There must be some trick, trap, mishap. It is always so. So, suspicious, this white-haired Swede rang down for a hotel messenger. He gave him certain instructions to be followed at once, and a large tip. Then he lay back in his bath, awaiting the messenger's return. Was the lady, in fact, a widow? Had she not some husband

likely to return? A possessive lover? A brother? Was she
a gambler's decoy? Or, most banal of all, was the Villa
de Bordighera no more than an establishment? This and
much else saw the soap over his body and the towel dry
off the water—while in the neighbourhood of the Rue
Buffa that hotel servant, himself a native of Nice, made
enquiries among the tradesfolk and the concierges.

Ohlsson had begun to linger over his toilet, losing faith
indeed, becoming every minute more carelessly certain
of the sort of answer he would shortly receive. But when
the messenger returned, it was to report that the lady
was a widow, returned recently from a year's seclusion in
the Dordogne, and now had lived for two weeks in the
Villa Bordighera, which she had rented for the winter and
spring. She was accompanied by one maid, otherwise she
lived alone. She had no friends in Nice, and had been seen
walking out only with her maid.

Ohlsson began hurriedly to look for his clothes, pull
at his collar; then saw how much time there still remained
and stopped; restless, went to the wardrobe and poured
himself a strong glass of brandy; with this he walked over
to the window and stood quietly sipping, considering his
good fortune and the wide indigo night.

In a clear, dark sky the moon had risen high, leaning
frothily on its side, ringed with gold. But what light it
gave was paled by the new night-lights of the town—
richly curtained rectangles in the Casino across the square,
yellow-green lanterns posted among carriages, the low
beams of automobiles, several whitish-purple letters spi-
dering the doors of awakening night-clubs. All day the
sun had beaten down direct, casting few shadows, greater
activity had seemed to exist in the sky than in the streets;
but now the sky was cool and asleep, and a new life rose
humming at street-level. Towards the sea, the palms cut

black-feathered figures, cruel as totems, against a sheet of calm silver. How different, Ohlsson thought, was this night-city to the sunny place in which he had spent the day; to the city of the sunset, an hour ago, when after tea for a moment they had stood on the promenade and watched the sky fire with pink and orange, while the sea had stretched out green as a milk of almonds—before the sudden emerald flash in the sky when it had all turned to violet, and greyed quickly into the night. And now this night-scene. Ohlsson, warm from his bath, cleanly warm in a fresh shirt, lit a cigarette and leaned forward from the warmth of his room to smell this night, to search for a fragrance to match the sounds and the view of night beginning. Then, his head out of the window, he shivered —it was cold. A sudden chestnut chill had risen with the moon, the air smelled of northern winter, his nostrils opened for the scent of wood-smoke; but no scent came, none at all; it was winter in the carnation city—and all that might faintly be sensed was the dust.

Suddenly, because of this chill, Ohlsson imagined the mistral. And then strangely his imagination, which should have dwelt upon happier things, drew for him a fearful picture. He saw the cruel curve of the long black palm-fronds, saw them swaying and leaning in the wind, beaten down; saw them one by one fly off, scything down to the square below, spinning like keen black scythes after the little figures of people hurrying home in the wind across the square. Each quick black scythe selected one figure, and in the night-music of the giant mistral lunged like rapacious fish, mowing off legs: other figures began to run, knowing their danger—they were all caught: some ran into the arcades, the palm-scythes scuttled after them into the dark arches with no sound at all above the singing, swingeing wind.

Ohlsson shuddered, shook his head—and for a second wondered why he had imagined such a scene. On such a beautiful calm night? After so perfect a day? With such fabulous favours in store? . . . Was he losing faith—did such preponderous beauty in itself invite destruction, a complement of calamity to balance and realize it? Perhaps the very knowledge of so much good fortune threw upon him personally a fear of disaster, a sense of guilt that he deserved no such fortune and that wrath must necessarily punish the fruit? However it was, he shuddered—and shuddering dropped his cigarette. He saw it leave his fingers, travel like a spark down to the street.

People's heads were passing. The cigarette fell somewhere—on a hat, in some nest of fur, into the lining of an open coat. Half in instinct to catch the cigarette, half from his heart to apologize, Ohlsson threw forward his hand, leaned far over the windowsill, peered with his head down into the night while his lips shouted "Sorry . . . ," leaned too far, overbalanced, clutched desperately at the windowsill but only clutched the beautiful indigo night—and then fell four storeys down to smash spread-eagled, bent like a dead starfish, on the stiff stone pavement.

People gathered round him, lifted his head, let it fall. All talked at once. One man who had no idea held his pulse. Nevertheless, he was alive, groaning. Soon the ambulance came. Later, in hospital, perhaps at some time between eight and ten o'clock, a broken spine was diagnosed. He had every chance of living, but little of ever walking again.

So years afterwards I met this man Ohlsson on the promenade at Nice wheeling along in his invalid-chair with its little streamlined wheels. We grew friendly, and he told me this story. Fingering the wet thumb of his cigar, he would smile and say: "That's why—I'm a fatalist." And at any rate, he would add, my back taught me to live more quietly, to think more calmly, so that I have written much that I would never have written otherwise, and thus the world has given me enough money to live comfortably in the sun, on this promenade, for which, understandably, I have a certain affection. And the lady? He never saw her again. She never knew the name of his hotel, had she wished to make enquiries; more probably she thought him some boorish adventurer who had found something better to do that night. For his part, he had not wished to inflict her with the bathos of his predicament. Yet he had been interested, most interested to discover how that night might otherwise have ended. It seemed, from cautious enquiries he made, that indeed it would have ended as he had hoped. During the next months the lady, it seems, had taken to herself several lovers; had married the last of these; had disappeared into the north.

LANDSCAPE WITH FIGURES

SNAKES occur. Some time ago in Padua a woman, sitting
in a café, felt the warmth of a friendly little dog against
her stockings. She reached down to pat it. But instead of
fur she felt the smooth cold leather of a snake's skin.
Impossible! For a moment—because after all, it was
simply that the snake had escaped a little from some local
zoo. Similarly, once a snake escaped from an animal ware-
house in London. It made its way at speed down the
length of the Tottenham Court Road, proceeded over
into Charing Cross Road, and thence in the same straight
determined line to Trafalgar Square and the Nelson
Monument, about whose plinth it was finally captured.
Then there was the thief who chose, among all the pockets
of the crowd, that of a zoological student: he drew forth
a thin, green grass-snake—non-poisonous, but none the
less a snake.

Milan: the Galleria Vittorio Emanuele II. The grand
shopping and lounging arcade that forms the favourite
rendezvous at the populous centre of this the greatest
commercial city and industrial nodus of the Republic.
Built in 1865, in times of kings. Glorified by a palatial
facade added in 1878. At the time, says Baedeker, it was
the most imposing shopping arcade in Europe. 'The form
is that of a Latin cross (640 ft. long, 47 ft. wide and 85 ft.
high), with an octagon in the centre, crowned at a height
of 157 ft. with a glass cupola. It is flanked with several
large café-restaurants, and is the favourite evening rendezvous of the Milanese.' Those, then, are the dimen-

sions—suggesting a building of considerable size and some intricacy. There is the name itself and other touches of period—a glimpse of great glass-and-iron cupolas, of all the plastered flamboyance of the nearing fin-de-siècle, of the glittering epaulette of Vittorio Emanuele II. Thus much in the book—but then comes the moment when at last, standing for the first time in exactly that renowned place, one asks oneself: What is this really like? How can one fix this for ever? How does it differ from the centres of other great cities? What are its colours, shapes, smells, sounds? And—passing from bare abstractions—what are its associative feelings? And who are its people?

Italy is at the same time one of the most backward and one of the most advanced of West European countries. What has gone forward has progressed at formidable speed; equally, much has lingered. Quite apart from the legacy of earlier centuries, one may taste the lyrical bombasts and prettinesses of the iron-clad nineteenth more purely in Italy than elsewhere. This is perhaps most apparent to the eye of a Londoner. For there remains so much of that Italy which was imported in quantity into late Victorian London, and has since formed for many the substance of a period more nostalgic even than childhood, the period immediately before one was born, the generation of parents, a time for ever unattainable but unmistakably close. In London—the mandolin tremolo of organ-grinders turning their Neapolitan street-songs, coloured-glass pictures of Vesuvius or Rapallo, the curtained windows of restaurants, pink-shaded table-lights that shadowed fly-blown wall-paintings of varnished blue seas: faces of the great black moustache on its double-barrelled chin, songs of gesture with short legs set firmly astride; the funeral and the joy of the love of large families; birds in a cage, confetti, macaroni, and the gilt lettering above shops that proclaim 'Italian Warehouseman.' All that, much more, and behind those contemporary lustres the paler classic ghosts of endless stucco terraces that lace London with Italy.

So in Milan one was charmed by meeting many of these ingredients face to face. And in this way too the great glass arcade, which by all other standards should have pained the eye, instead charmed. Æsthetically hideous, it contains nevertheless the magnificence and the nostalgic echo to be sensed in great hothouses, beneath the roofs of a railway terminus. An atmosphere to be sensed slowly, over fine iced coffee, as on that particular evening, an evening in early September, of which this account tells.

Sitting on one side of the central octagon, one could see in several directions along the broad vistas. It must have been nine o'clock, a breathless warm evening, and the people were beginning to stroll after dinner. Silk, one felt —a lot of silk, and much fanning. Heat weighed on the air, everywhere one caught sight of a hand that seemed to flutter, to beckon, yet really held a paper or a fan to snatch a moment's draught from the close air; silk—for one was in the greatest silk-centre of Europe, and everywhere glimpses of the lustrous soft stuff flowed pale over dark skins, silk of dresses and shirts and handkerchiefs. Straw panamas, white coats, thin suits, sandals—these textures gave the passing Milanese a coolness to which the arcades themselves lent their own stately sensation of draught. For the high glass domes echoed, very slightly, every sound—there is a coolness of escape in an echo. The very height of the canopies gave a sense of freedom greater than in the open street—a high roof puts a measure on space, figures beneath it walk smaller than beneath the measureless sky. The floors were of stone, cool stone, dustless and suggesting draught. Yet for all this loftiness, for all the motionless festooning of plaster volute and caryatid that climbed so high over the drab-coloured walls to the dome, there was no real draught: it was close, high summer, a night for iced drinks, for fanning, for eau-de-Cologne. The scent of eau-de-Cologne and pomade hung everywhere—sweet, but not hot, a reminder that one seldom sees an Italian skin sweat. Dry-skinned, smiling their cool white teeth, sparkling an elegant energy, never listless, the people sauntered or stood in groups, talked at the café tables, sipped their lemonades and ices. At their level the shop windows glittered freshly, and the restaurants shone with a golden clean electric glow. Several bands played at various cafés. Everywhere a chattering echoed. And at that moment, even then perhaps, the snake was moving itself restlessly in its box in the zoological gardens a kilometre away, uncoiling slowly, raising its sharp head in search.

Of course, although one still felt this to be less a contemporary scene than something from opera buffa, although there still shone the pink shirt and the grey bow tie, and old men with white moustaches passed in broad black hats—the eye at shop level was accosted constantly by the soft modernities of metropolitan Italy. Through the doors of one café could be seen the brilliant edifice of a chromium ice-making machine, on a wall nearby glowed blue neon bars advertising Strega, a faded white dog painted on a shuttered window spoke in pale vermilion letters of 'La voce del Padrone.' Several women, although it was long past sundown, still sat beetle-eyed in sunglasses. The chairs of one café were made of little steel sticks. At another café there blew, glorious in peroxide and pyjamas of viridian satin, a ladies' jazz band.

Part of the crowd had gathered to stand and watch these ladies perform. Here at least one knew the purpose of the

passers-by. Ordinarily such a purpose is difficult to assess
—everyone is bound on intimate errands of their own:
the small muttering man in a straw hat hurrying across
from the Scala, looking to neither side, disappearing at
the opposite end into the broad cathedral square; three
carefully pomaded young men, avid for every girl who
passes, strong-eyed and taunting with their laughter, who
are joined by their mothers and an elderly gentleman; all
those who passed with bent heads, intent on no one knew
what, all those others whose sauntering held a secret
meaning and who all possessed lives and homes and
directions. But those who stood by the ladies' band were
simpler—they had come to listen to music free, to look at
other people drinking free, to partake at a foot's remove
of the mondane gaieties—they were those without lire to
spend. They stood in a crescent round the café, only a few
inches from people sitting at their ease—yet quite at ease,
prepared to stand for a long time, unmindful it seemed
of those more fortunate than themselves. Whenever the
band came to the end of a tune, they applauded as loudly
as the true clients at the tables—and the lady-leader bowed
to them as much as to her nearer guests. In spite of
frayed shirts and working belts, in spite of heavy winter
trousers, there was still an immaculacy in the appearance
of these the poorer but no less oiled. All were virile types
of a fine-looking race proud of the grace of their bodies.
Among the younger men there stood few women. But
many old men watched, proud still, but saddened—those
who had seen other Italies and who now had fallen with
the lira. Many of these must have travelled that evening
from the outskirts of the city, drawn in by the central
parade. Many must have come pounding down the broad
avenues in the great green Milanese trams; between the
enormous blocks of flats and offices, modern and here

magnificent; along the triumphal way where, at that moment, that snake from the zoological gardens would have been selecting his secretive gutter, a direct gutter-way to the Piazza della Scala and the Arcades. Though perhaps it had chosen instead the smaller darker streets, more anonymous paths snaking to the rear pile of the great stone cathedral. At least, no one saw it.

The ladies played with energy and allure. Six sat, the leading lady swayed in front with a long gold saxophone; but those sitting often stood up to trumpet their enticing solo; and all the time they rose and fell on their seats—small gilt cubes the size and shape of rostra for performing animals—like a posse of trotting dragoons. Helmeted thus too, for though most must have been dark, their hair in every case was bleached to brittle silver-gold—so that each wore above swarthy eyes a metal helmet as burnished as the saxophones and trumpets. They played jazz music in a jumpy, ladylike way—no dark African drawling for them, each piece became a kind of picnic for Italian teddy-bears. But they played with Latin attack—with the gusto that rattles a fast tune at the pace of a chariot race, with adagio that weights the drum-beat of a slow melody with painful misericord. Whenever for a moment one or the other laid down her instrument, her lips knew no respite, their pursing broke into instant smiles, wide allurements of white teeth and red lip—and then it was curious to see what odd designs the kiss of their instruments had made on the moulded lipstick. They were a ladies' band—at the end of each piece they all began instantly to chatter to one another; sometimes it seemed that the music interrupted one long conversation, in the way that the anecdotes of telephone operators are broken by thoughtless calls.

But these jaunty gold and green ladies were not the only performers. For in front of the crowd of onlookers, in the small space before the tables started, there jigged to and fro a short, wild-eyed man with a piece of chalk. He walked with a shuffling broken jig, laughing, sneering, breaking into rhetorical appeal; but his main performance was with the chalk. He raised this significantly, brandished it, then threw himself to his knees and inscribed carefully on the stone pavement 'Abasso . . .' Abasso this or that, the government or the premier, taxes or prices. The pavement was covered with these marks. No one interrupted him. No one took him seriously. Sometimes they tittered. Though no doubt he was doing his cause a certain local harm—he was having a very good time himself.

The other performers played in the night outside—one an unseen scuffling and shouting somewhere along the street, perhaps some brawl in a bar. The other was the weather. When all had seemed so placid, there had been a silent massing of clouds. Now these began to creak with lightning and grumble a sullen thunder on to the hot air. Small sudden winds breathed through the arcade. One looked up—and abruptly an intricacy of high iron ribs showed in the glass roof as that blue lightning flashed its great sky-space above. The storm asserted itself tremendously on the quiet warm air of such a still Lombardian evening: vividly, as in no northern country, one felt the great arc of the sky menacing its rage above the lighted arcade, above what must have looked a bubble gleam of glass to those high night-fighters of the storm.

It began to rain. The air cooled. People hurried in from the street. The chattering rose, everyone at once must have said: 'It's raining.' As on all rainy nights, the sounds of the city far outside were amplified—unheard before, train-whistles and the grinding of far trams linked the enclosed arcade with the streets. The Galleria took on a new life; the leisurely brilliance of the evening was swamped with movement that recalled more the morning arcade, when those covered pavements became the venue of free marketeers and every kind of swift exchange. But meanwhile unconcerned the ladies played on, the great coffee and ice-machines steamed and glistened, the neon and electric evening glowed on beneath the shuddering sudden blue fire from above.

Then suddenly it seemed that there had been a cloud-burst; that the glass above had crumbled; that some new elemental ferocity was clearing one length of the arcade. Miraculously the massed passers-by had vanished—crowd-ing into cafés whose doors were now banged shut, melting away in diverse directions like water itself. Scramblings, overturnings of tables, shrill cries heard even above the thunderclap. But one sensed rather than heard the move-ment, the sudden emptying provided a vacuum stronger than a sound, the pause of an arrested clock.

One length of the arcade was absolutely deserted. But along the very centre, in the wide space between the tables to either side, magnified far beyond its size, a small move-ment occurred. Gliding over the stones in a very straight line, moving slowly and easily, there travelled a snake, a fat brown cobra. It made directly towards the crowd round the band. A head turned. Another, and another. Small cries, a scream, a susurration of the word 'Serpe! Serpe!' That crowd was gone. Those at the tables, too, they all packed out to the cathedral square. . . . But then stopped, as if protected by the dividing threshold. Shout-ing and gesticulating, rained upon and suddenly alive in the lightning, they watched the snake assume the place where they had stood. It paused at an aisle between the tables—and faced the ladies' band.

Now indeed there were only four ladies left—three had

seen the snake and had instantly bolted. They might have screamed 'Serpe!' at that time . . . but the others had not perhaps seen or heard, or had concentrated the more on their instruments to keep the music going, not quickly understanding that what the others had screamed was a truth. But now, straight in front of them, five yards away up the open aisle, paused between two tubular green chairs, lay the long writhing of that brown snake. Its head pointed at them. It had hardly paused, seemed only to be gathering its long glittering coils into position for another glide forward. Thus the lady-leader must have seen it—it was plain from a sudden stutter of her saxophone when she did. But she never moved. She never stopped playing. And the three still behind her played on, though plainly in some senses paralysed. Their eyes had left the frets and the keyboard and were stuck on the snake, but they followed her lead and continued automatically to play.

One has been in theatres struck and theatres nearly struck by bombs. After a pause of paralysis—as though some clockwork mechanism has been arrested—the players continue without concern their play. Those in the audience as one person rise in their seats, as if the first chords of an anthem have sounded, and then for want of space to throw themselves anywhere, as one person subside and go on watching the performance. In a theatre that catches fire panic must similarly be avoided—and it is traditional that the orchestra strikes up panic-averting music. Just so now, from somewhere deep in her professional mind, that lady-leader might have taken the decision to play on; or perhaps she felt that the snake had approached too near, that the time for flight was over; or perhaps she was simply hypnotized. But most likely it was the tradition. She no longer swayed. She stood rigid as a priestess. Above her head a neon sign for Cognac

blazed steadily, another to the side announced 'Gelati.'
Over all the lightning threw its fitful shock, sudden
shadow and bright light.

Then almost in that same first second of recognition
there happened a fantastic trick of fortune. The coincidence that only happens in real life; that which must
never appear in a novel or a play—in those confections
where only certain characters mentioned must have their
effects upon one another, and no outside agent, as often
happens in life, and happens increasingly as modern life
becomes more diverse and less parochial, may interfere.
But no human agent interfered here. It was a coincidence
of understandings, of action and mistake, of misunder-
standing. For though now the lady-leader continued to
play without pause, errors and stutterings occurred in the
melody, many of the notes were mislaid; and with faults
in harmony from the others, the sound emitted took on
remarkable qualities—there were echoes of the atonal
scale, the scale of eastern pipes.

The snake's head began to rise. Held backwards, its
eyes fixed on the saxophone, the slim brain seemed poised
in thought, or in search for thought, as though it tried to
remember something once heard long ago . . . the head
rose higher, extending as though out of itself, with the
fearful sinuous movement of all worm creatures. Then held
erect on the tower of itself, plinthed on its circled length,
it began to sway from side to side, with eyes fixed solidly
on the musician statuesque a few yards away.

And that lady! Those ladies behind her! Their fingers
devoured the keys, they hurried, hurried, but always
stayed stuck in the same bright-lit café shop-window!
Soon the leading lady, she who with bleached hair and in
electric-green satin pyjamas remained upright—she too
began to sway. Slightly, definitely, she swayed her shoul-

97

ders and her long gold horn to the snake's motion; their four eyes, hers and the snake's, seemed thus bound together by unseen wires; together they swayed like two men adrift in a drunken discussion. The lady thus by chance appeared to behave the more normally, for with the rhythm of the music the saxophonist keeps up just such a shifting sway.

But only normal on the surface—she was rigid within; and the fact of its happening there, just there in the terribly empty arcade, petrified further the scene. For a place ordinarily so alive with movement, with crowds, with sounds and purposes—this emptiness in itself would have appalled. Its plate-glass refracted with no flicker the yellow electric brightness. Varnished woodworks and gilt traceries and the many polished painted things about stared as furniture stares in a funeral parlour. All was life—but with no movement, deadly still. The orange-and-blue neon bars spoke their words—to no one. The polished stone pavement lay smooth and swept and clean—for the passing of no one. The café chairs sat prised at angles—welcoming no one. The great glass box simply waited, bright with unease; like a room seen in a mirror, like an exhibition before opening; like a deserted museum; like a place swept by a plague so secret that no one dared breathe a word of it, not even to themselves—no one brought themselves to switch out the dreadful lights. That would have been enough—but now in one corner stood that group of shocked figures spangled with green satin, with the barren glitter of instrument and hair, with lip-rouge red, giving out into the emptiness a queer warped music, chorus after chorus, a dirge atonal as a figure distorted in queer mirrors, played emptily and ceaselessly, never for a moment pausing, again and again, chorus after chorus.

In each fifty-foot high portal of the gallery the on-lookers pressed thickly against the invisible barrier of their fear. Rain still fell—a light rain, rustling with small movement; rustling like the continual whispering of the people themselves, who never ceased to talk, though now in whispers and undertones held down by the suspense of what they saw. Only now and again a single shout rang out, as in one or another the excitement had to escape. One man—of the kind who assumes natural leadership—shouted repeatedly at intervals: "Keep on, keep on! The keepers are on their way! We've telephoned the Zoo! Keep on!" Quite near to him stood the little man with the chalk—sometimes he attempted a half-hearted jig, muttered his 'Abasso,' but always stopped and returned his fascinated eyes to the islanded band. And once a young man, excited and vain, broke the ranks and crept towards the snake, a stick in his hand. Half-way he paused, hesi-tated, shrugged his shoulders, opened his hands palm-upwards to the crowd ('What would be the use?') and returned, excusing himself victoriously.

By chance, this man's gesture and another feature of the scene were both reminiscent of the bull-ring in Madrid. There are many differences between the Span-iard and the Italian, but some things they hold in common. For instance, they can be brave as fire when with roused blood they are convinced of a cause; but otherwise, when common sense suggests a merit in survival, they may easily run—the better to live to fight another day. Never-theless, the gesture of bravery is made. The aficionado of the bull-ring will suddenly jump the barrier, race across the ring towards the bull, brandishing a square of red handkerchief; then turn tail and, with wild cries of triumph, exalted suddenly by a stroke of reason, return manfully to the barrier. So that young Italian returned, loud with excuses, thinking: 'Absurd! Why take such a risk? For what reason? For a ladies' band? Are there not hundreds of ladies' bands? Are they my sisters? Do I even know them? Did I pay a single lira to hear them? Was I in the café? Mother of God, I've nothing to do with them at all.' The other memory of Madrid flickered from the brassy gold of the leader's bleached hair; for, sitting high up and looking down on the splendid perspective of the tiered crowd and the arena, the most vivid motive of all that brilliant panorama, brighter than the blue sky and the yellow sand, the gilded costumes of the toreadors and the glistening red splashes on the bull, was always the amazing glitter of sun-flashed gold that sparked from a thousand bleached señoras packed in the tiers below.

A scuffling began behind the crowd. Then an opening appeared automatically, clearly and suddenly—the keepers came striding through.

With calm accuracy they walked straight through and directly to the back of the snake, noosed sticks in hand. A deft lassoing, a grab along the back of the head—the snake was caught, boxed in a lead-looking box. Such awful efficiency appalled. It brought with it no cheer, but a sigh of wonder, perhaps of disappointment. There was revealed instantly the cold logic of the whole episode, a logic that matched heavily the bright vacancy of the arcade itself, that weighed heavily on the charged air. That the escaped cobra should seek shelter from the unaccustomed night-streets and the weather in a dry glass edifice reminiscent of zoo-houses; that it should be faced by a figure erect and frightening; that then it should play at being charmed—erect and on the defensive, not listening to the music though so the story goes and so it looks, but instead swaying on its elected defensive; that the ladies, cornered, should assume so traditional a rôle; that the keepers should come so calmly to reclaim their hooded treasure.

It seemed suddenly all as empty as a straight line. But then the lady-leader toppled over in a white faint. And the man who once had crept forward now rose to his greatest height, raced forward, issued instructions in a loud voice, frowned, gesticulated, appealed, ordered, claimed absolutely the body of the sprawled blonde. His arm round her raised shoulders, her head flopped on his protection, he came haphazardly, perfectly, musically, to the retrievement of himself and his own.

THREE DOGS OF SIENA

THE Italians love their dogs. And their dogs love the Italians—it is probably to show something of this love that these dogs take such care to reproduce themselves, not in the dull matrix of formal breed, but in most brilliant assortment, in a profusion of wild and unpredictable shape ever a surprise and a joy to their delighted masters. What we would call the 'mongrels' of Italy are more than an essay in democratic procreation: they are an unceasing pleasure to the eye of those who love the individual, the purely creative rather than the creatively pure, the fresh. Not only joy but genius distinguishes this variety. Nowhere but on the ancient peninsula famed for its fecundity in noble and inventive works could such hounds occur.

One day three such dogs arrived in the Tuscan town of Siena. 'Taken for a visit?' they would have said, 'And who is taking whom?' For so full of joy and industry were these fortunate dogs that in everything they preceded their masters, running always forward, smelling out the fresh ground first. Their names—it turned out later—were Enrico, Osvaldo and Fa. They came from Naples, Genoa and Venice. They were owned by three brothers resident in those cities, who now for a period had come to be reunited in Siena, the town of their birth, for the wedding of their younger sister. However, names are poor descriptions for such dogs. They must be studied in all particular, observed in the detail of their spectacular creation. First, Enrico.

Enrico was a dark-brown dog, almost Umbrian—

though he came in fact from the yellow Neapolitan quays. Stoutly built and heavy, he was not tall enough for his broad body—though muscular legs supported firmly this solid barrel. The brown hair grew short in tough whorls on his back, but down from his chest and stomach it hung sternly shaggy. His face was his great glory—it was nearly the face of a mandrill. Thick-snouted, bristling with what at first seemed disapproval, it proclaimed the thinker, yet a tough thinker, ruminant but muscular for the fight. His eyes were pale liver-coloured, with bluish rims that circled them completely; but very often one could see nothing of his eyes, nor could he himself see quite where he was going, for a heavy shag sprouted from between two ears the shape of small oast-houses and sprang forward in a wave like one great bristling didactic eyebrow. In a curious way this eyebrow seemed to part as it fell on to his snout proper, and to either side it combed away, becoming a beard to drink up Enrico's strong slavering. At the other end—it was a good way—there occurred the stump of a thick rat-like tail bent backwards and curled up sharply to its bitten spatulate; this revealed perhaps too boldly a bare posterior, hairless again as a mandrill, and not too well-looking—but possibly this was not Enrico's fault; possibly he never knew quite how it looked, it was so far away.

Fa came from Venice, his fur was white as his native Istrian marble. He was a fluffy dog, always laughing. At first sight one took him for a Pomeranian—he had all the powder-puff fur and bright black eyes, ever-pricked ears and slender trotting legs. This at first—but then as in a dream, or in some distorting mirror, one saw that all these pretty characters were strangely exaggerated; the white fur sprouted like a clown's frill; the little legs spun so thin and delicate that in motion little Fa seemed to travel

on wheels; the inquisitive ears rose inches high, like
paper squills. But his tail was Fa's greatest pride—instead
of a fur ball this joyful member flowered into a high
spreading fan, beautiful but overweighted as the sail of a
felucca, and as such particularly helpful with a following
wind. However, Fa's was perhaps mostly an eccentricity
of character. His laugh, his perpetual busy trot, his ever-
bright eye and his spirited soprano bark singled him out
always as the life and soul of any street, a true lover of life.
He liked often to walk on three feet. He was so called
after the fourth phonetic of the singing scale, having
arrived at a similar stage in a litter of eight.

Osvaldo—Osvaldo could claim in his way to be the
finest of the three, if one spoke of earthly finery, of the
feathers that make the bird. A big dog, by and large
Osvaldo had grown to be the shape of a hyena—his front
shoulders rose several inches higher than his tapering
thin haunches. But such haunches never slinked, Osvaldo was no cur, that slendering was meant for speed.
In other ways too he seemed contrived for speed—his
long wolf-like nose thrust streamlined forward; his ears
grew huge and round, the trumpet ears of a flying-fox;
his grey body was covered with tan-coloured spots, so
that such a fur had some of the look of feathers, like the
feathery pelt of some griffin-beast from a wilder world;
and his tail fled away in a long streak—though normally
he carried it curled. But his eyes! His eyes were bright
yellow, as yellow as a leopard's! These it must have been
that gave him, for all his speed, such a strange impassive
expression. Never the glimmer of a laugh, never a message
of anger could be sensed from that motionless face. One
never knew what he thought. He seemed away with his
yellow eyes on the far horizon. Genoa had been his birth-
place.

The three had first met in Florence. They had become instant friends. Florence had been selected as a convenient junction for Siena, and a most pleasurable few hours must there have been spent between the platforms and a nearby restaurant. They had then taken an afternoon train for Siena, a train of good wooden carriages, and had arrived after dark. So that on their first night in the hill-town the three dogs had not had the chance to see anything of their new home—though the journey in the fading summer light had offered many pleasing prospects. The dark lines of cypress outside Florence had proved interesting, a pleasant strolling place where many enquiries might be satisfied; all over the low, unexhausting hills these trees had occurred, in competitive groups or singly, like darts thrown at random into the brown earth by a fond divinity. Then, as the earth turned redder and Siena approached, there came the strange perspective of the vines, each planted singly, twisted helter-skelter figures, intertwined and loving, but statuesque, arrested in movement and in no way disquietening to the interested dog. But to Siena itself they arrived enclosed in the dark carriage—it proved quite a drive from the station to the higher town walled on its crest of hill. They had spent the night comfortably enough enclosed in a small yard. The gate had been locked, and nothing of the precincts could be seen.

The next day dawned warm and sunny; the air was filled with fresh smells from the good Tuscan earth. This not only proclaimed the joys of country life, but indicated also that there had been a day or two's rain recently—so now the weather would be fine. Good weather, then— and a new town to explore. At breakfast there had been one small drawback—the remains of a pasta flavoured with dull tomato sauce instead of the good meat gravy of

Bologna. But who knew what the bins and gutters of this place might provide, a town known to be centred in rich, fertile country? At last the gates were opened, and the three friends stood sniffing on the threshold of their new adventure.

But not much time was spent standing still! A second only for three noses to appraise the air, a glance to left and right—and they were racing off. However, as is often the case, that first dash was little more than its explosive gesture—in fact they all ran in different directions, noses to the ground, and instantly circled back to the gateway. It was a ritual—and now fleet Osvaldo, betraying in his yellow eyes nothing of his intentions, took charge and wheeled the party off along the road to the left—uphill. Mandrill-faced Enrico plodded his muscles behind. Little Fa became a brisk third, though sometimes he ran forward and completed a circle round Enrico. They travelled at a lively trot, searching the sidewalls as they went.

The road led steeply upwards between tall houses of red brick. It was narrow, a kerbless street of a kind they must all have known—the cobbles met with clean precision the dark-red perpendicular of the walls. But for a time—such indeed was the precision of the Sienese mason—one might have thought this the precinct of some well-ordered private mansion. No debris littered the stones, no stones nor brick nor plaster had fallen from those well-kept walls. Nor were there any projections of any kind—no door-steps, door-posts, lamp-posts, trees—nothing that might invite the pause for consideration. Iron torch-brackets occurred frequently, but these had been placed too high for practical purposes; and the graceful architects had moulded those surrounds to their doorways so neatly that nothing obtruded, no pilaster jutted from the fine-fitted frames.

Then shops occurred—and shops could never occur in private passages. But such ordered self-contained shops! What sort of town was this? They grew uneasy. As the industrious file plodded on, they passed not a single bin, no brushed pile of warm refuse. The sober red-bricked mediæval streets wound narrowly up and down, arched and turreted, with never a buttressed invitation—not grim, but richly grave, precise and cleaned as no town they had ever known. Frowning behind his forward hair, Enrico must have remembered the alleys of Naples, redolent of life and all odour. Osvaldo's fox-like ears would have trembled to the unheard echo of the bustling Genoese arcades. Small Fa's great tail fanned blindly for the warm resistance of all those exudations that thickened the air above the green canal by which once he had lived.

But what was it they sought, truly, bowling along at such urgent speed, sometimes on three legs, sometimes cavorting dangerously sideways, frisking and plunging— yet always continuing forward, in what was plainly an agreed single file, with searching nose and rolling wary eye? Certainly it was not, in the main, food. Nor was it another matter that, with such stores as they had retained carefully for this expedition, must have weighed heavily. It was something deeper. It was without doubt the need to find evidence of their own existence.

This they could do only through the help of others. The search for food is automatic. But the urgent cry for testimony is a different affair. A dog alone in a stone street might well wonder whether he existed, the sus-picion that he was no dog could breed dangerously among the dry mirrorless stones. What proof was there? To glance down at a paw, to whip round one's head at a remote, diffident tail? What did that prove? After a moment of illusion, of pleasant relief . . . nothing. Naturally one's dog brain attributed to itself paws and tail, fur and flank; but—how be sure that this was no deception? Impossible. Proof must be sought elsewhere: it could be found only in the movements and essences of others, the clash with unfamiliar bodies and with feelings foreign to one's own intimate brain. These others were at best other dogs, but other creatures would do—cats, men, and in a more distant fashion the rats and small bodies of one's prey.

Suddenly Osvaldo stopped dead, feathery front legs splayed stiff, his fishlong snout sniffing upwards, yellow eyes peering at the wall above, fox-ears primed for intelligence. Enrico and Fa bowled to a halt and stood quivering. But they never looked up. Instead they gazed from side to side, sometimes glanced anxiously at Osvaldo, but above all pretended not to notice anything extraordinary. Here was etiquette—a pronouncement would come in good time. They stood like dogs that pause suddenly in the middle of a game, panting, abruptly indifferent to each other . . . yet patently pretending this.

High up on the wall was set a stone tablet. Sculptured in relief, Osvaldo saw the effigy of a large woman-dog with sow-like udders nourishing two naked human children who squatted beneath. He stood peering curiously. What could this mean—were the dogs here magically transformed into humans, was it another feature of this strange town? A glint of unease showed in his yellow eye as, turning his nose rather away in embarrassment, his fixed pupil revealed a thin crescent of the bluish-white. Romulus and Remus, ancient colophon of Siena, sat drinking above, impassive, cherubic, unconcerned with the passing of new wolves.

One has seen dogs pause in question before mirrors; or grow startled at the sight of an unaccustomed object—a parasol, a tall hat. Some bridle at the phantom of blue spectacles, others growl at the movement of a rag flying in the breeze. What in fact do they see—what do they *know*? Their eyes are never more alert, the finest intelligences are cocked in their ears—a certain uneasiness underlies. Perhaps an instinct, long lost to our human systems, perceives emanations of evil (we know that such instincts exist, as with the polarization in a dog travelling over unknown distances back to a former home). Or perhaps once it has been frightened by something looking the same—though in this case such a selection is queer, it balks at a parasol and disregards a walking-stick, and this only on certain days. Or does a keen appreciation of the angles of light—which again we have lost—describe around the object an abstract image of some unfavourable beast? Certainly the dog that sees himself in mirrors—and only in certain mirrors—behaves as if this might be so. He does not imagine as we do that he sees himself. What more likely he suspects is the presence, the significance, and so the threat of an alien that bears upon his own life. From his mood, his cautious sniffing and startled eye, he shows not outright alarm but suspicion and unease. His attitude is like that of the man, say, who sees written before him the words 'good and evil.' Suddenly he notices how this is almost exactly 'God and Devil.' The blood rushes to his head. Letters the same! Meaning the same! He stumbles for the dictionary of etymologies. And then the appalling truth is learned—all four words spring from different roots, it is nothing but coincidence! But this, staring at the words, he cannot really believe. Science has explained it. But for him, staring still uneasily from the sides of his eyes at these words, there is still suspicion; around his thought flutter birds of great significance, for a long time he will remain uneasy. In such a way Osvaldo looked up at Romulus and Remus. He must have known the wolf was not real—but he had his suspicions, he felt not sure.

And if this indeed was the case—what bewilderment Siena held in store for him! What a distracting plethora of porcupines and elephants, giraffes and unicorns and all those others that form the signs of the seventeen Sienese districts, and which everywhere are emblazoned in chivalric colour on the red walls. But, of course, this was not to be—though much worse threatened these unfortunate dogs. For the moment Osvaldo gave one deep growl and then—as they will—suddenly lost all interest. He appeared suddenly to forget what he was doing—and glanced curiously at the street itself, waking from a daydream. Then wheeled and was off at a trot. The others tossed their heads, seemed to jump as excitedly as if this were the first intimation of a walk that they had ever received, and followed. They disappeared round a corner.

In a town as small as Siena, we who moved constantly about the marvellous streets of course kept meeting other such industrious walkers. Those three dogs seemed to occur everywhere. More than the little girl with the bird-cage who gave out printed fortune slips, more even than the mournful young man with a black eye and his arm in a sling who must have been much knocked about in the recent Palio. The Palio, furious horse-race galloped in mediæval costume round the Campo of Siena, had been over a week. The crowds had departed, the tempers of the various districts or contrade that competed had cooled —for this annual race was as fiercely contested as it was picturesque; it was no show for tourists, but a traditional trial of strength between the contrade, as alive now as when first, centuries ago, it had grown into being; the jockeys with their round helmets thrashed each other as freely as they thrashed their ponies, bribery and tricks and competitive tempers rose high.

But now the parades, processions and pageantry of the great day were a week over—though there still remained certain ceremony to be completed. Now and again one saw bands of Sienese dressed in mediæval clothes come drumming up the streets. Contrary to what might have been expected, this distinctive people dressed up so carried no feeling of the operette: they looked real, conclusively. In their stripes and scalloping they marched against walls of dusky red, dark old true walls—each man's face was a face seen in a mediæval painting. The brownish, ochreous faces were unchanged—and in themselves they were as distinctive from other Italian types as, for instance, are the people of Arles from others in South France. A feeling of pride and fine breeding is sensed. And here they lived in a town that was as preserved as their traditions and their own bodies. A town austere but mellow—kinder than Florence, yet as with many such mediæval cities resonant of the sense of death. Well-preserved in its graven self—and also well-kept from day to day . . . its clean stone streets contrasted strongly with the streets of other cities. One wondered, again idly, what the three dogs thought about it. And soon, as if we had called them, though the town was really too small to count it a coincidence, they appeared. Suddenly racing down under an arch into the main square, the shell-shaped Campo.

Industrious as ever, they travelled fast. Noses to the ground, heads tossing, tails and behinds wagging separately like the afterbodies of ants or rumba dancers.

That was their way of coursing the streets—but here, here suddenly striking into the magnificent open ground of the Campo, they skidded to a halt, stupefied. Enrico and Osvaldo stood sniffing the space like incurrent lions, while small Fa bounced to and fro between them on his stick legs, a small messenger between those larger craft. What—whatever could be going on in such ever-searching minds? Had they seen and stopped stupefied at the sight of the seventy or eighty marble posts that ringed the course of the Campo? Had such sudden generosity in this reserved city overwhelmed them? Had Enrico glanced up for a moment at the blue sky and seen rising, rocketing up against it, the tremendously high campanile? This delicate square tower of dark-red brick, so slender in proportion to its needling height and the vertiginous pale castellations bulging heavily at its far summit—this most beautiful erection of man that seemed ever to be moving upwards, which seemed in fact to be flying, rocketing, spearing itself in vertical flight into the wheeling heavens, this so vertical tower that gave us a glimpse that the world is round—what did it signify to Enrico's liver-coloured eye, suspicious through the hair-mop? Could his wondering, almost-intelligent mind have registered its proportion, so that it appeared to him as a giant pillar, an exquisition too great for him, but of the right shape and thus innately satisfying? Worldly as he must be, Enrico turned his head down again to the cobbles, the nearer posts of rough stone that ringed the Campo—but there might, there might have been a glimpse of understanding in that second's attention, a possibility that was borne out by what later we were to see, in the episode that finally unseated these furry ones.

Now, they hastily addressed themselves to the first of the posts—and then continued round the fan of the racetrack, rehearsing their own intimate Palio. Unspoken words seemed to circulate between them. No barking, but rolls of the eye—the whites of their eyes rolled like those of negroes against the coloured fur, while Fa's black jets gleamed with a dark, clownish radiance—rolls of the eye that seemed instantly to be understood, indicating a different direction or a different post, and above all a call to industrious joyful companionship. Episodes and encounters marked their progress. Here at the hub of the town more was likely to happen— although the Campo itself, because of its curious tilted shape and its quiet historical recession, seemed always more deserted than other Italian squares. Nevertheless at one point Enrico, running along, was seen suddenly to wheel; he returned nosing to what he had nearly passed— a scrap of ham-rind left like miraculous manna by the sweepers. His pace had nearly taken him beyond it, but that square-nostriled mandrill nose had saved him. Now he settled his mouth down to the scrap, and with mournful eyes began to eat. As he munched the pupils were raised thoughtfully, showing a lugubrious droop of white beneath, and those whole eyes, stricken with the conscience of sin, moved slowly from side to side. He was like a man weighed with sorrow—or a child doing what he knew was wrong. In some curious way he seemed to be listening to his stomach. It was notable that this was the one occasion when the news of a discovery was not circulated to the others.

But the others! The others had found at last a brother animal—not one but two, a brother each. Osvaldo had found a cat, and Fa had looked up suddenly to find a dog sitting almost invisible in a dark doorway. Fa abruptly stiffened—shocked, outraged. He raised his small self to what he must have imagined was a monstrous size.

On the points of his paws, on inexorably stiffened legs, with neck erect and eyes implacably averted, he walked up and down quivering in front of this sitting Sienese dog. It was an exhibition of outrage, cold outrage. The Sienese, fat and well-groomed and almost well-bred, took no notice whatever.

With Osvaldo it was different; perhaps because his meeting was with a cat. And such a cat—fat, sleek, striped, heraldic! The dogs of Italy do not chase cats like their brash northern brothers. There was no reason for the cat to do other than continue to sit and gaze across the Campo—with imperturbable placidity that must have seemed remarkable to the excitable Genoese. That huge dark-striped cat, in the erect posture of some heraldic beast, simply sat and considered the Campo. Osvaldo stood opposite, his head hung, his paw half-raised, blinking his yellow eyes uncertainly. In Genoa the cats were lean and thin-jawed; their kittens were as meagre as large mice; they moved all the time, creeping and slinking. Nothing was more different than this well-fed, gloss-coated monster.

But in neither case could anything be done, the Sienese animals made no move whatsoever. Finally, Osvaldo turned away, shaken, from his cat; and Fa made longer and longer circles away from his dog, so that soon he could appear to walk away naturally, unconcerned. Enrico alone had profited—and that not overmuch, the rind had been tough and salt.

Such, then, were the minor encounters of these three eager lovers of life. Before the following day, we saw them again twice: once down by one of the town's gates, down past a long pink wall surmounted with leaves green against the blue, where one saw the town end unencumbered by suburbs, and the gentle dark-ribbed patchwork of the Tuscan fields map out to the horizon beyond; where those dogs had found two other dogs making love, and as dogs will, were circling the indifferent couple with excited sallies and a jabber of barks—animated as the chatter at a tea-party on the mention of human love. And again we saw them, of all things, trooping out from the cathedral door, industriously pacing the marble mosaics, disappointed and possibly ejected from that extraordinary hall, having no interest in the lofty rows of popes' heads, the graven fruit decorations and the striped totem pillars that give that place a cold exotism, as of a tufted African village frozen into stone. No, they were not to be touched by such ceremonies of stone—they went in search of life.

The next day they found it. Some time in the late afternoon we were at the hotel window, looking out on to an odd interjunction of roads running at different levels that complicated pleasantly the view. Of these, the main road was embanked, and thus passed slightly above eye-level from our window, while a short gully of steps descended from it to the lower street beneath. Presently as if it were a matter of course, the three dogs came pounding in their ceaseless single file up the lower road. And at the same moment, from along the upper road, came the sound of a kettle-drum and marching feet.

The dogs heard it, erected their ears, faltered and stopped. From where they stood they could see nothing of the upper road, they could only hear the marching feet, which now came to a halt, and the kettle-drum which ceased to tap and began a long, mounting, death-like roll. They stood there listening—it was plain they did not like what they heard. Enrico and Osvaldo stood with tongues lolling, panting quietly, heads lowered listening;

Enrico's shaggy forehead appeared furrowed with thought, listening for some unpalatable truth; Osvaldo searched blindly with his visionary eyes, but his lowered head seemed to be waiting for the whip to fall. Fa stood erect, tremendously rigid, his small pink tongue pouting straight out forward—at first sight one thought he might be wild with laughter. Meanwhile, we could see what in fact continued on the upper road. A group of the Porcupine Ward, the Istrice, had come marching with flags towards their votive church and had stationed themselves there on the way to perform a Sbandierata, a flourish of flags.

The drummer had planted himself, feet astride and firm, in the centre of the road. With implacable elbows he drew from the drum its ceaseless coil of sound, ever more rigid, ever growling out a greater power. Four or five of the others had stationed themselves at intervals along the road. These men carried standards, flowing white flags of great width, upon which were emblazoned patterns and the dark effigy of a crouching porcupine: these flags they twisted in the air with graceful mastery. Each man wore a parti-coloured black-and-white mediæval jacket and hose; each wore a mediæval cap, and showed thus underneath a grave clear-shaped mediæval face; the quarterings and stripes of black and white, splendid colours of the dark-red city, showed bravely against walls of that ubiquitous dark burning.

In all principal elements there was nothing in that scene to suggest that the centuries had passed—suddenly in front of one on the everyday street, in the sunlight, was flashed the flesh-and-blood mediæval happening. The clothes did not behave as stage properties, muscles rippled within them and the bodies were filled with the true blood. With strong grace they wielded the heavy

flags, twisting and furling and swinging them above their
heads, slewing them down to the ground like cabers,
hanging back against their weight and deftly manipu-
lating their hands in a music of equipoise and inspired
motion. The huge banners swam through the air like
coloured winds, like bubbling swathing smoke, viscose
heavy elements beautiful on the moving air. Fiercely
toothed patterns sprang into being, vanished in a sweeping furl. A porcupine appeared high above, sat for a
moment in chivalric splendour, vanished. All the whole
flags and their staffs were tossed suddenly high up, as if
they themselves leapt, hesitated in the upper air, sank
down more slowly into the hands of the standard-bearer.
Then again great circles—and still from the drum a
constant drumming, the drumming never ceased. It
seemed as though the flags themselves were alive and
trying to wrestle away like wild birds from their athletic
captors. It was a battle between flags and men.

Windows had opened, heads had appeared. Several
passers-by had paused to watch. But these did not disturb the truth of that scene, they themselves were the
anachronisms, a drab intrusion upon the splendid brick
and the bright designs of livery. The pageant succeeded:
a small gilt procession will triumph over mundane
crowds—but here, by how much more was their success
achieved! Then, of course, we saw that other intruders
were at work. The dogs. Osvaldo was climbing the steps.

He took one look, drew back crouching—gave a
whelp of fright, and loped shivering down the steps, tail
between trailing legs. The others looked at him sharply,
sadly.

A pause—it seemed for reflection, for necessary in-
decision. Then carefully, slowly, with a hesitation that
never quite asserted itself, the three of them, no longer in

single file but abreast, climbed the steps. They stopped
before the top. Below the very last step they stopped, and
stood there furtively pointing their noses over the top,
as if it were a parapet: small Fa had to raise himself on
two legs. Six uneasy eyes flickered with distrust as they
watched the flags; one recognized the germ of hysteria.
What they saw could not have been flags—but great
wrestling coloured shapes pouncing on the wind, zoom-
ing low over the men that fought them. Nothing quite
similar had been seen before: except, though much
smaller, in the shape of birds.

Were these then giant birds of fierce colour that had
descended in droves upon the town, sharp of beak and
horrid-eyed? Remorseless, lidless, steel-eyed birds?
Eagle-giants to tear out the vitals, thrusters and squaw-
kers, great feathered bolts of muscle and iron claw, divers
and risers, vile destroyers of gravity? Bones and feathers
and cruelty—but as for feathers, one could not quite see,
they flickered and furled so swiftly: were they snakes,
was it fire, or worse—animated sharp-teethed cloths,
living cloths headless and limbless, savage with consuming life, unclean and unknown? . . . Whatever this
was, it had never before been seen, it was dangerous.
And there was no smell.

On rolled the nerve-searing drums, the dogs stood
still—poised to move in two directions at once. They
were stretched—by their legs and tails lowered and
moving backwards, by their noses extended forward to
draw in the air with anxious sniffs. Their eyes showed
the white; and because they were interested and thus
grew lively, appeared again most considering, wise,
intelligent. Patricians' careful eyes they cast on those
unearthly flags—and then, as nothing happened, as the
flags made no attack, they took courage. Enrico—as if he

were taking the pipe from his gruff and bearded muzzle—
gave a low growl. One could not hear this for the drums,
but the sound could be seen vibrating his body, one
lip was raised. And Fa, propping himself alongside, heard
it, heard it as a sign, realized the mounting of confidence,
and quickly, in his excitable way, raised his muzzle in a
peppering of short white barks. Osvaldo continued to
stare with nerveless yellow eyes—and then presently he
too raised his long nose into a position almost vertical,
like the elevation of a sky-gun, and set up a long, un-
broken howl.

The flags swooped and tossed, bellied and swirled in
the rising sbandierata; the drummer's elbows held their
noise in an iron grip; the dogs mounted their howls and
barking in chorus. But a deadlock is never satisfactory for
the lively ones. One cannot stay still—any action is
preferable, backwards or forwards. And these three dogs
from the sea could no longer contain themselves. Buttressed with barking, their confidence rose—and suddenly as one they raced forward at the nearest flag. It was
circling low on the ground, they tore at its swiftly-moving
swathe—and got their faces soundly lashed; for a moment
they were lost, enveloped, blinded in a fog of silk; then
up fled the great banner and circled thrashing at the
higher air, the dogs crouched dazed—and then they were
leaping at it, throwing themselves high like bags of limp
dog, snapping, snarling, barking their last breath.

They looked then like three sacks erratically bouncing
—Fa's white ball moving faster but lower than the larger
brown two others. Ears well back, eyes quick with long
white fury, teeth open, they gathered themselves and
leapt at the enormous bird threatening from above. This
was no plaything—they fought hysterically. One knew it
instantly when for a moment the flag circled lower and

menaced, with no illusions of dogged valour, for a second they cowed back guarding themselves ... and meanwhile the standard-bearers plied their flags, they had no time in their exertion to watch the dogs. Nevertheless, the ritual of the sbandierata dictated that soon the banners should descend. The dogs leapt higher.

The Italians love their dogs as they love life—but they also love ceremony, and in all ceremony there is the touch of death. The will to live may also be the will to die. Whether it is a rite of harvest or marriage or church, death resides somewhere in the pomp, the order, the finality—and what is always a sense of immolation. All life for the time is suspended, a pause in living comes to revere the solemn act. There prevails an echo of all past sacrifice, solemnly one remembers the many years this rite has been preserved over the graves of others. There is an awe in the very finality resident in ceremony—all completion is a symbol and desire of death. A city such as Siena, grave and crenellated, stony and austere beyond its sun-warmed colour, is hung around with the cold breath of dead, glorious history. Other cities, as Naples, can bear their past differently, can vibrate with life so much that their time-scarred ground, repository of the ancients, seems the more fertile for its buried old ghosts, and death is so fortuitous and facile a part of the daily struggle that it is neither welcomed nor revered. But not so Siena, the quieter, cleaner, graver city of mediæval calm.

The drummer suddenly shook his head to one of the people watching. This man took the message and dashed forward, doubled up, to kick Osvaldo sharply on his bony flank. Osvaldo gave a yelp, looked round astonished at this man, hesitated—wondered why he had been attacked; was he not in battle for a brother man against the dangerous bird? And then receiving another kick, slunk sorrowly away to the side of the street. Enrico was dealt with similarly—small Fa saw what was coming and followed.

They sat in a doorway, framed by the severe stone lintel. Their eyes glanced with apprehension at the drummer, at those watching; the kicks had not hurt, but the meaning was absolute. Sometimes their heads turned to the flags and revolved with them. In a nearby doorway sat a Sienese cat, well-fed, tranquil, heraldic. It seemed at last that Osvaldo, Enrico and Fa had assumed some of the same sedentary pose. They seemed to be considering the fatal words, that breath of the worm that says: 'Perhaps it is time to settle down. . . .' Contentedly to die.

When a minute later the sbandierata was over and the drumming group marched away and was lost along that narrow street, they were still sitting there. Life, it seemed, was over; trotting was done. No more now but to sit in doorways, to sit and wait. Calmly to await the cold breath. They had been touched by the city, they had been permitted to see beyond the veil. No more to do but wait, satisfied, content, half-dead already.

PASTORALE

ONE first heard a sound like low-toned cowbells, like many cowbells crushed and chorded together—and then round the narrow corner of old grey walls nosed the chromium grill, the long bonnet, and then all the pale gleaming length of a torpedo-shaped roadster. It wheeled noiselessly, thick-tyred, up the soft earth street, and stopped at the centre of the village. That was not far, the whole squat clump of the inner village hardly extended more than four of its lengths round the long automobile. But how it took charge of the graven, shabby place! Each house was built thickly of dark rock, windows were so small that one noticed no curtains—and the irregular street, rather a space between houses than a street, was all brown beaten earth, with a few cobbles, a slash of crumbling tar. Grey and dust-brown—the colour of the mules that sometimes trudged through like white-lipped old fools.

Against such earthen textures the pearl-pale car shone with a princely lustre; the chromium flashed precious silver, the clean canvas of its hood sat reefed like Parisian cloth, the luggage of yellow pigskin and gold clasps told the tale of Pullman seats and luxury. At the wheel sat a young, lean, dark man; the sun flashed on his oiled hair, on the platinum watch glittering from his soft glove, on the white card he now studied. The woman at his side, her face like a soft white nut in its rich brown hat, peered over—and then, with eyes screwed, looked up at the house above in disbelief.

I thought that they must have been given an intro-

duction to the pension, perhaps from the Syndicat d'Initiative back at Ajaccio. This mountain village, Piana, lay
half-way up the jagged coast; one needed a recommenda-
tion. I was about to call down to Madame Paolo that there
were customers—when through the lace curtains I saw
that old black cormorant already bustling about the car,
bowing and smiling, tugging at the luggage; she must
have been at her own window below minutes before me,
shadowy eyes rapacious behind the curtain. The man and
woman hoisted themselves out of the car; the seats were
set low; it was an effort to haul oneself out from such a
comfortable car, the woman showed much awkwardly
opened leg. But this in no way discomfited the peasant
boys, who stood absorbed with respect at such new-
arrived wonders. The couple never paused to wish these
onlookers a good day, they seemed not to see them. But
when Madame Paolo tried to lift a big suitcase, the man
smiled pleasantly and took it from her.

A little later, it must have been four o'clock, I went
downstairs to the parlour that served as both dining-room
and entrance hall. The man and woman were sitting at
one of the tables, drinking coffee and goat's milk. Neither
looked up as I came down the bare wooden stairs. It was
a small room, holding three large tables, and draped about
with a curious assortment of art-nouveau and early-jazz
ornaments left long ago by forgotten commercial travellers from France. It had a very closed-in atmosphere.
It would have been difficult to imagine any estrangement
between strangers in such a room—but neither of these
too looked up as I came down. Nor when I asked through
the kitchen door for my own coffee and chestnut cake.
When Madame Paolo brought this she walked round to
the other table and asked whether they required anything
more; the man answered politely, but impersonally, and

had turned back to his coffee while Madame Paolo was still smiling. In such rooms, in a strange village, and with all the mountains and rolling maquis wild outside, it is exceedingly difficult to remain impersonal. One is in a shelter more than a lodging-house.

Since they were so firmly absorbed in one another, I could watch them quite closely. This was not comfortable, the atmosphere was so aloof; but certainly one could feel no fear of indiscretion. At length it occurred to me what probably they were—and what they did prove to be: they were a couple sufficiently young in marriage still to be interested in themselves beyond any other person. Not so young as to feel themselves performers; not old enough to wish for others to perform.

One has seen them everywhere in hotel lounges, or in one's home-town masquerading as one's friends. In the hotel lounge they sit together in their armchairs, he turning over the pages of a book, she with a writing-pad on her knees. They never speak, but one senses from them a stronger air of intimacy than from all others in the lounge. They never look up at other people. They are absolutely incurious about the world without them. Older couples will show the searching eyes of escape. Unmarried people will be searching for immurement. But these two will sit solid, an affectionate brother and sister arranging some funeral visit; but how warm, how enviable a funeral— how armoured, wonderful! And as for those who pretend still to be one's friends—see them, for instance, as hosts at dinner. Watch them exchange private messages of the eyes, grow silent as they dismiss the conversation to speak anxiously of some intimate affair of their building which has been growing at the backs of their minds throughout dinner, watch them spring to their feet as you, the old friend, apologize for the need to leave early. And how enviable their glance as the door closes, how real the small things they will say—deeper than all the first passionate words. And how empty one's back feels—walking away from the eyeless smiles, wishing even for the lance of malice, but receiving from them nothing, absolutely nothing. . . .

In this case, their evident prosperity increased such an armour. In mainland towns it would not have so obtruded; but here on the poorer island such prosperity fired into magnificence, their rich leather and tweed looked soft and fabulously of the town. One inferred immediately that the man must have something sinister in his dealings—but really, he could have been a well-off young merchant or professional man who had looked after his money. He was a lean man, dark-eyed, polished in his tweeds as a Parisian; manicured, muscular, silk-tied. The woman sat smooth and plastered in on to herself, in the sheath of her dress, in her close-set hair; nowhere a strand astray, but fired here and there with a jewel, and with over this smoothness a loose coat draped and askew to proclaim ease, to accentuate what sat tight and unruffled within. They sat silently drinking their coffee, looking for the most part down at the table, at their hands, or to the furniture a foot on either side. They spoke little—at first glance one would have considered them unbearably tired of each other. But when they did speak—they looked straight into each other's eyes, without flinching, pulling no false expression! They smiled without laughing, without twitching! They neither raised their voices nor kept them low! When the woman asked for a cigarette, she took it without thanking him: yet he was thanked.

Outside the weather was bright and fine, a hot November sun mixed with the clear high air and the breeze of

autumn. No mountain chill, only a deep invigoration—
like a cool old wine, a yellow wine. I walked out by the
church, a rounded plaster basilica washed pale and sudden pink against the grim grey of the other village buildings; old men, moustached and corduroyed, sat smoking
on benches against the wide circular end of the church—
through the day they moved round slowly, as on a wheel,
with the sun. I climbed up the road, then took a hill-path.
It was steep, one mounted quickly. It was a path and a
brook combined, so that upwards one trudged from stone
to stone with the mountain water coursing down in between. Very soon the village lay far below. One saw the
roofs huddling in round the church—in that broad,
sharp mountainscape like a huddle of sheep round their
pink shepherd, pathetic, blind, but nuzzling safe.

A climb of ten minutes on those slopes brings out the
heat and sweat, and already the country is as wild as anywhere farther. I saw a mound of moss and brush and
climbed off the path on to it; once there had been a stone
goat-pen there, and the old circle of stones remained, a
curious fairy-ring, and good to sit on. The ground was
thick with dark olive moss, above the great chestnut
woods blazed yellow up the mountain, below the green
maquis of cystus and sweet-smelling scrub stretched down
and down, past Piana, to the eucalyptus groves by the
warm sea—to Porto, little port for the loading of chestnuts, cork and granite. All was vegetated, mountains
thickly carpeted with a smell of herbs and the rich brown
taste of chestnuts. Occasionally a small wood of arbutus
pricked the green with scarlet berries; far above rose the
mauve mountain-tops, beneath stretched the wide and
lovely blue of Porto's gulf, ridged with red stone. All the
time I could still see that polished car and its tailored
companions.

They must, I thought, be from the mainland, motoring
from Ajaccio right up the coast to Calvi. At Calvi, sleek
with yachts from Cannes, they would come to rest in their
grand hotel of balconies and bathrooms. What, I wondered, would they think when they found there was not
even a bucket in the pension, nothing at all to be done but
wander into the chestnut woods with one's copy of the
Sampiero? Then I remembered their armour—of course
this would protect them. Nothing could disturb such
equanimity. They would smile, remember that the journey
was being broken only for one night, and indeed wander
out into the chestnut woods—with perhaps a copy of *Le
Temps*. That was in itself a small matter—but it suggested again the exasperating notion of that armour, their
carapace of incuriosity against which no one in the world
could prevail. *No one*—the absolute quality of such
armour frightened. Here was something at last impec-
cable, a dreadful example of the perfection that man is
supposed never to achieve. Indeed, it might not be
constant, there was the certainty that time would corrupt
it ... but nevertheless for a time, and perhaps for as
concrete a time as a year or two years, their state would
remain an immaculate truth. Evanescence may be a
condition of life, but against this generality there is the
real measure of time—minutes, hours, years. Pleasure
for a year is more desirable than for a minute; so, more
valuable. What the two had, for all present purposes, was
a solid armour. Nothing would undo them. Accident,
malice, affection, the chestnut wood—they were proof
against each eventuality. Lawyers might write their
letters of doom—they would look at each other, inter-
telegraph their two-ness, and then deal with matters,
unsuccessfully or not, it made no difference. Friends
might deliver their invitations, they would nod their

dual head—and know that the friends would get no little piece of them, not one fragment, they would go only to come back.

And of course they would be favoured by systems—I was walking back downhill to Piana again, having the idea to walk through the village and beyond to the Calanches, to watch again that sonorous eruption of red rock, a landscape unique in Europe—by simple systems and habits. By their clothes one could judge that they were part of a set section of society. There would be behaviour permitted and things not done, standards that would aid considerably the impulse of agreement; many questions would never be posed, originalities of wish would not have to be agreed—nodding was made easy. They would not, of course, be proof against small disagreements, rows of the ruffled nerve—but these would soon be straightened out: the disagreement would never include anyone or anything else. They would suffer neither jealousy nor envy, nor any desire for escape; such rows would be physical, nervous reflexes, headaches essentially within the armour.

I passed the car, now in shade, but still gleaming. What would they be doing upstairs in the bare whitewashed bedroom? It was difficult to imagine them making love, they looked too intimate. But in fact they would have been satisfied often and well with each other —or the armour would have creaked. So upstairs above their car, while the leather travelling clock and the ivory hairbrushes sat quite still on the dressing-table, they might have been doing whatever they wished? Writing letters—each was as evidently sensible as the other in the case of these two, how could one interfere, even to guess?

The road out of the village became a first-class cliff

motor-road, snaking about round a deep gorge, but neatly walled and smoothly surfaced. It was quite a walk to the Calanches, and as one travelled this road—intensely alone in such a wild geography, as alone as the ringing of one's boots—the sea opened far out down to the left. It was not, of course, miles or even far—it was the illusion of distance seen from a height. Now the broad sea with its corrugation of hair-size wrinkles looked like blue beaten steel, like the steel of a lacquered fire-iron: away out a large white cloud drifted, hanging down two vicious white tails that tried to be waterspouts. Ahead lay the Calanches. A quarter of an hour later I was among them.

Here the vegetation to either side ceased—one walked along a road suspended between precipitous cliffs of fierce red granite, a steep convulsion of weird rock that seemed to glow still with the fire of its first spawning. This was a dead land, a canyon, but on one side open frequently to the far-down echoing sea. Promontories of dreamlike twisted red rock towered away down to that sea, gulches and gullies dreaded down to the great blue gulf—and each one of ten thousand pinnacles of rock was smoothly sculpted into a strange hooded shape. Holes and sockets stared as though blown by the wind, whistling silently with siren invocation. Nothing moved. All those fantastic sculptures stood still—coy tourists simpered that one looked like an elephant, that another was for all the world a bear—but they were in fact simply figures, figures standing inevitably as themselves and nothing more, figures deep in thought about themselves, their stone thoughts cowled and draped with red stone, ponderously waiting for motion. An æolian music sang round them, but it was too ancient a sound for human ears.

For human ears! But there, along the road leaning on the wall and watching this vast colloquy of still stone souls, stood two soft humans, tweeded and diamonded, but nevertheless soft skinfuls of flesh, those two of the contented car! They stood watching the sun sink on the Calanches, close in their companionship, proofed in their tegument of quiet passion. Theirs were no linked hands, no leaning and pressing together of bodies that searched for the other's comfort—they could stand side by side, with the cool air between them, sure of each other's presence and affection and without need for the flesh of reassurance. And then the sun with remarkable swiftness changed its golden blue for red, for gilt red reflective of hot coral and the branding iron. The sea turned purple, great stretches of olive milk appeared—and above the sky darkened, and began to shine with the phosphorescences of night; but overpowering everything, the Calanches started to glow, to burn, to blaze with hot red light. Now all those standing figures, those pinnacles of graven thought took on deep shadows—burning red themselves with projected movement, invested with misery, black shadows under their eyeless cowls and tapering behind them. One felt the sea itself would steam for the immersion of these sad hot creatures; ice-green lichens that here and there occurred were burnt up and vanished in the broad consuming glow.

Alone thus with the rock and the sea stood the two whom nothing could assail. As the sun sank farther, the contortion upwards of all that rock showed itself more plainly—here suddenly was a vista such as Blake drew, a thousand souls in anguish moving upwards, the silence now a mute chorus of despair, each cowl griefed and crying.

But I had been wrong. Their armour was not immaculate, those two were town-dwellers. The woman straightened herself, and gave a little shiver. They turned to each other, their eyes must have met, they seemed to hunch their shoulders and then hurried quickly away, back walking fast to the car, to the safety of their room.

AFTERNOON

IPPOLITO was employed in the Boboli Garden, Niccolo in
the Pitti Palace—both, in their different ways, as keepers.
For many years between these two old men there had
existed a scornful, yet temperate, feud. Perhaps the air of
Florence, and of the broader Tuscan quietude, had kept
their passions thus in check. In fiercer country or in more
striving towns, in the Vesuvian chaos or the Milanese
swift order—whims might have swollen to passion and
bred a dark and sunny violence. But Tuscany is temperate.
Grim, ancient, fertile, gentle, the flowering of its princely
genius is over, it has worn itself out, it has decided not to
crumble, but to sleep away into recession. Clothed in
monastic calm, it has entered its own tranquil cell. There
is everywhere the touch of death, but none of the will to
die—the air of the cypresses that stalk Fiesole. And
another life-force to temper the grimly fortified prison-
mansions, there breathes still among the little hills a panic
queerness as strange as the slant-eyed, point-eared
Etruscans who in ancient times trod the vanishing woods.

Temperate then; and thus the more extraordinary that
the feud between Ippolito and Niccolo finally ended in
violence. Though this was by no means a conscious
violence—but rather the attack that can breed itself from
humour, when the slight cruelty behind a joke swells
suddenly, like the extended plumage of an angered bird,
and with savage beak strikes. One never knows when this
will happen. Nor did old Niccolo when, it seemed inno-
cently enough, one day he won some few thousand lire
in a lottery.

But first the previous events of this mild affair must be remembered. Its mildness indeed was such that the original cause had long been forgotten. Whenever either of the two old men tried to call this to mind—and it was not often, the feud was intermittent, they only suffered their antipathy when they came face to face—they supplied only possible reasons. Sometimes Niccolo, who came from the hills round Volterra, ascribed it to references that Ippolito, a Roman, had made to his rusticity. At other times he thought it was due to a quarrel over a favoured seat in a small café which Niccolo considered his own and which one evening Ippolito had by chance entered. Then there was the question of a certain rich and most generous American—both men had tried to make his own part of the Palace sound to the American more interesting, and there was a deep suspicion bred whenever this gentleman left Niccolo's hands for the welcome of Ippolito in the gardens, or Ippolito's for the crafty words of Niccolo on the polished palace floor. And in the same way, for his part Ippolito would remember sometimes the rounded figure and warm dark moustache of a certain lady who served behind a bar on the way to the bridge across which, on the other side of the Arno, they both had their homes; but this lady had long ago disappeared. Or had it been a dispute on the renewal of uniforms? Or shock when one day, in desecration of the years, siding himself with the betrayal of dearly loved traditions, Niccolo had suddenly shaved off his great grey whiskers? . . . Neither could be sure. Such small events themselves stood out sharply only because they were isolated in the calm of so many years. More probably the two men had conceived some broader antipathy—something in their appearances not easily to be explained, nor to be analysed from their characters, which were in both cases ordinarily congenial. However, there it was—and often when they happened to see each other they would hasten to show their mutual contempt.

Ice and fire both blister, strong hates are like strong loves. Possibly, in the marriage of opposites, the lesser degrees of dislike and attachment are also indivisible. The two old fellows might really have rather loved one another. Certainly, whenever they met their interest quickened. For instance, if they happened to be included in some general discussion, each automatically took an opposite side, forgot the generality of the subject, and spoke only to and at each other. Another rivalry was of a regimental nature. Niccolo, who had a faunlike face and thin upstanding ears, who was an old satyr from Volterra, had spent years under the green cock-feathers of the Bersaglieri. Ippolito, thick-necked short bull from the Romagna, had served his time in an ordinary, but stolid, regiment of foot. So that often at the sight of Niccolo, Ippolito would raise his voice in the crowing of a cock, as many Italians do when the Bersaglieri strut by with green cock-feathers flying in the wind of their quicktime march. To which Niccolo would reply by making a decisive gesture to his backside—in honour of the day, largely rumoured, when Ippolito's regiment had once turned tail in battle and received the enemy's fire conspicuously in the rear.

And sometimes Niccolo, with a half-hour to spare, would wander out through a back-door in the Palace, climb the long walk of the gardens, looking for Ippolito. Then, pretending not to see him, he would by mistake stumble against some precious plant, knock his pipe out on the nose of a surprised stone statue, or even—most absently—spit into the fish-pond, when the lively fishes would swarm nibbling at this unexpected feast. All such devices were loudly execrated by Ippolito, limping angrily up the path, waving away the intruder with his arms.

Niccolo would look startled, confess his thoughtlessness, and with delighted eyes apologize. Later, Ippolito would have his own back—walking on to the clean Pitti floors with the garden mud on his boots, or directing visitors into the private entrance of the custodians—thus discovering Niccolo uncapped and at his undignified ease. Such were the sallies that distinguished their mild feud— small sallies, in small spite, infrequent, in no deadly earnest. For long periods all was quiet between the two. They were minor, inconstant eruptions.

The day came when Niccolo won his little sum at the lottery. A few thousand lire, but a windfall for the custodian—whose wages were low and seemed never to keep up with the inflated prices of those difficult years. Consequently, that same evening he invited his wife and several relatives to a café some distance from his own home, which stood in one of the small streets by the Bargello; he thought it would be a change to visit a finer café, a café on a big square, though not too expensive— and he chose the wide and lively Piazza San Maria Novella. By chance, this was Ippolito's district. But neither then nor later that evening did he see Ippolito. However, the broad Piazza, with its thin green gardens, its ice-cream stalls, its busy small trams and the tall black-and-white marble façade of its church far, far across on the other side—these might have reminded him of the friend of his irritation.

They sat in the open, on the broad pavement; the piazza shone alive with electric light—from open café doors, from high-wired street lamps that hung like moons above the passers-by, from all the windows of hotels and shops round the extensive square. Above these busy illuminations a clear moonlit night stretched its quiet and distant dome; but one was not looking at the night, one's eyes were on the level of trams and melon-sellers; on the white-coated bar-tender bending over his great zabaione machine, whose mechanical whisks whined into the marsala and egg like dentist drills. Machines like these everywhere—the great chromium ice-cream and coffee industry whirred in the angry neon glare; huge trans-Italian buses packed high with luggage swooped their monster radiators between the trams and bicycles; illuminated advertisements sharpened the hot night air, hygienic white surfaces covered the bars, white-coated dark-haired attendants serviced dexterously their machines and drinks. The Italian genius for mechanics, the legacy of minds like Leonardo's, triumphed everywhere. Ubiquitous energy— no sloth. And wonderfully the machines whirred side by side with sellers of hand-made Sicilian hokey-pokey, by the leisurely wicker chair, by the mule-cart passing, by green shrubs and old walls. Comfort and the conversational evening survived, the Italians controlled their machines. But of course Niccolo took most of this for granted—though suddenly his eyes were held by a sight common enough in Florence, but which must then have stimulated in him the seed of an idea.

Already, before meeting his wife and the other black-dressed relatives who now sat clustered round him, he had drunk a bottle of wine to himself. At dinner nearly another, and now these amplitudes and the coffee he sipped induced a mood from which he could look on the world with benevolent criticism. Thus his attention was struck by two or three boys, ragged and barefoot, aged not more than ten or eleven, who scuttled continually under the legs of the outer fringe of café tables. On their faces, hard with premature age but still of angelic set, faces of lean angels who have somehow suffered a passion long before their turn, there blazed the holy light of search; round

their necks were hung satchels made of sacking; these
bulged already, the evening or the day perhaps had gone
well. The boys were gathering the tin tops of beer and
mineral-water bottles. These the waiters tossed anywhere,
so that naturally a fine scattering had gathered under the
inner tables too—not only on the outer fringe.

These further treasures the boys, bent, saw. And soon
they were scrambling with the ease of dogs right in among
the human legs and the table legs. But they had none of
the sensitivity of dogs, and their energy was such that
short of upsetting the tables themselves they managed to
buffet and almost unseat many of the people sitting there.
Niccolo saw this—and laughed. It was amusing to see the
life in the young rascals. There had been days, long years
ago, when he himself had been brought by his family on
visits to Florence and . . . but suddenly his dream was
interrupted, the thought of Ippolito had suddenly crossed
his mind, there appeared a connection between the boys
and Ippolito—and then as a preposterous idea emerged
a great curved smile broke his tough old faun's face, his
ears seemed to slant back against their cropped hair, his
eyes gleamed queerly.

He waited till the boys drew near. Then abruptly he
reached down a hand and grabbed the shirt of the first
boy who came scrambling beneath his chair. The boy
tried to wrestle, but Niccolo quickly shook his head and
whispered something. The boy hesitated, not quite be-
lieving, then listened again as Niccolo muttered at him.
How much did he get for his bagful? So and so a kilo?
How would he like to be paid twice as much? He and his
friends? When? Now! . . . And Niccolo smiling his faun's
smile brought from his pocket a sheaf of large Italian
notes. The boy's eyes widened—but he still maintained
an angelic calm, the submissive tranquillity in those taught

to beg young. Niccolo's wife leant over to snatch the notes away. He reproved her—this was private business; no, he was giving nothing away. His wife subsided, shaking her head, and then stayed watching him like a dark glitter-eyed bird. But Niccolo had already forgotten her and was explaining something to the boy.

To the suffering angel-face he explained that he would buy his bag of stoppers and all those of his friends for twice the price they ordinarily received, More than that— he wanted then only the use of them for a half-hour, after which he would return them to the boys. They could then take the stoppers away again and resell them at the original price! In this way they would be paid three times over!

The boy's eyes looked—almost with reproach—at the money. It must have seemed so near, yet he dared not touch it. And Niccolo was speaking again, this time with his finger raised. There was a condition. The deal should not be transacted then. Instead the boys should come to the Pitti Palace to-morrow and ask for him, Signor Niccolo Morelli, custodian. There, without fail, the deal should be transacted. The angel gritted his teeth, concentrated. Reluctantly, then voraciously, he agreed. Niccolo named the time. The boy scrambled off.

Thenceforth the evening was spent pleasantly over coffee and small glasses of liqueur, without further event.

The next afternoon was hot; Florence lay becalmed in the brown arrested waves of the Tuscan hills, dozed in an August doldrum. No cloud in a sky as still and dark blue as a painted postcard, no scent of moisture in the hard, dry, crumbling earth. Blue above, lower a dry green of trees, and lowest the sun-greyed brown of baked earth. Ippolito stood half-way up the broad steep central walk

of his Boboli Garden. He had climbed slowly, now paused
for breath and looked down to the great rusticated palace
lying lion-dull below. Its rocky masonry and its firm
windows nestled low, framed on either side by dark-
green descending hedges. Gravel and moss, cropped grass
and the graven amphitheatre of statues and stone urns lay
in between. No flowers, no water. The fountain there was
dry. Old Ippolito took off his black stiff cap and drew a
hand over the brown bald back of his head. As often on
these hot days, he looked with envy at the Palace, at the
stone walls so cool within. Like a sailor longing for the
land, the old garden-keeper longed for the polished,
smooth, dustless floors of stone. Just in fact as many
times as, imprisoned within the stone, Niccolo the custodian stood gazing out through lifeless tall windows at
the grasses and tempting leafy walks of the earth-smelling
garden; born of the country, he longed for the mysteries
of dark walks and the sun-shafted foliage, the eerie living
growth of gardens. But both men were chained to their
separate work, there could be no interchange. Nor did
they ever express such a desire. Only at moments they
felt a longing—with Ippolito the longing for rest and the
comforts of man-made sanctuary, with Niccolo a yearning
for the ancient woods. So now Ippolito, having simply
for a moment enjoyed the coolness of his mind's eye,
grunted and turned up the walk again. To either side lay
the entrances to shady paths, paths set squarely in the
high dark-leaved hedge, moss-cool paths where sudden
figures of sunlight emphasized the darkness. But Ippolito
continued straight towards the top.

This was the circular apex of the garden, where a
fountain still played, where in a round stone pond fish
swam out their cool circular lives. From the gradient walk
it could be seen only as an upper horizon, a plateau where

the steepness ended and the nearer sky promised a high freshness. But when one had completed the ascent—there was only the flatland, one had arrived not on a point but on a plateau, and banked higher still there were trees that circled against the sky. However, these trees were small, and over their short tops the sky appeared, only the sky, and this gave an illusion of space—as with the sense of broad stretching land reflected in sky touched by a hedge top. But Ippolito sensed such things only vaguely; tired, old, stiff, hot, he stood on the plateau and looked round with his professional eye. A man was sweeping plane-leaves that had already in early August fallen and turned brown. A girl was lying on a stone bench, her skirt askew with sleep—well, he would walk over and correct her in a few minutes; it was a long way round. A nurse passed slowly with two children—they had touched a bronze statue and were excited that it had felt so hot, so hot that it stung. And these few people—no one else had climbed the hill in such a fierce heat—all kept to the shade. The wide stone pond and its gravel path burned in the glare.

Ippolito lowered himself for a moment to a stone bench—then abruptly sat upright. There, among the trees to the other side of the circle, stood Niccolo; and he was talking to three small boys. Why wasn't he down in the Palace? Who gave these palace keepers time off to do as they please? And why—which was a more logical curiosity—had the old fool troubled to walk up that baking hill in the August heat? Just then Niccolo stooped and pointed towards the fountain. He held in his hand what looked like a sack, or several small sacks. Ippolito stiffened further—he disliked any interest of the custodian's in his precious cool fishes, he knew it led often to trouble; Niccolo had no love for solemn order, his was a wild eye with gardens.

Then the boys broke out from the shade and on to the path—three ragged boys from the streets bobbing excitedly in the sunlight. Niccolo followed, shuffling as fast as he could. The gardener sat tense. Anger rose in him as he saw Niccolo's shape now clearly. And the three of them went straight for the fountain pond, the boys jumping and shouting round Niccolo like an uncle. Niccolo reached into one of his bags—he drew out a handful of something and threw it straight in the pond. Food? Fishfood? Poison? . . . But already the boys were over the parapet and dancing about in the shallow water, diving down, looking for things, picking things up, scattering the fish, shrieking the afternoon with their cries! The gardener was off his bench with a grunt of rage.

Already that old faun had reached in his sacks again, he was scattering more things farther round the pond. The boys still pecked with their hands in the first place. Ippolito reached them and shook his two fists at arm's length, swinging his arms like an old windmill. The boys turned, stared, laughed, ignored him, splashed farther on. Ippolito raged beyond the parapet, looked at the water, placed a foot on the stone, then decided not—instead he shuffled off round towards where Niccolo stood laughing outright and throwing more things in. Bottle-tops! Glinting, frilled bottle-tops—metal!

He raged up to the custodian. But this was no Niccolo of the mocking apology, this time there was no stopping him, he was away with his laughter. And now over the broad pond the boys were scattered, splashing and treading everywhere. Ippolito went right up to the other's face and gesticulated, letting the curses stream from his mouth. The fishes would be poisoned! The fishes would die! The directors would see! Sacrilege to the gardens—was there no more order? Stop it, halt now—or he would personally protest to the Board! What was he doing out of the palace; was there in the palace no work for ridiculous old clowns, corrupters of the young, hooligans, criminals? On and on he raved, gesticulating into that other's face queerly gripped with laughing. His hands struggled wide like the wings of a great bird that would never rise. They fluttered close, gripped in electric shock. They opened to lift invisible painful weights. But still the face laughed on.

Laughing eyes stretched to thinner slants, his mouth fixed in a goatish V, his nose thick between joined eyebrows and beaking then down with unholy intention; the old olive grizzled skin wine-red with laughter, his stomach cramped so that his knees crouched like an animal's shanks. Such a face clear-cut in the breathless afternoon pause, under a still sky, against the shimmering light ground and the black shade of trees; for those hours the very trees seemed to pause in their growing, the panic hours when an afternoon presence is abroad. On top of such a face the black-peaked cap sat incongruous, crowning.

In all his years then Ippolito drew back his hand to strike. But somehow contained himself—by sense, or perhaps drawn by sudden new cries coming from the pool. The other two children, the children with the nurse, had jumped in! The nurse came up panting, bleating to either side, to unseen people, as she ran. The ragged boys shrieked at the new children, robbers of their stoppers. A splashing battle began. They fought, one boy fell, then another into the water. The still surface of the pond was whipped erratic with waves, the children plunged about muddily embroiled in a silver spray.

Order was Ippolito's first command; it was too much, he was down at his boots and unstrapping them. Out came

his feet, white and vulnerable on the hot hard ground—
then he was in the pond, paddling after the boys. He got
one by the ragged collar and jerked him to the edge and
out. He went for another, by that time like an eel the first
was back. One after the other he got them out, always
they squirmed back. The nurse kept one, but more was
too much. The still air cut with cries, Niccolo stood alone,
crouched helpless laughing, the nurse kept up a hennish
outraged flow. Such noise, such muddle, such a squabbling
knot in so much stillness—that girl lay still asleep on the
bench, and all around and below Florence dozed out its
noon—until hot and struggling and bemused old Ippolito
had got beyond trying to capture the boys and was himself furiously reaching his hand in the water and slime
and picking out the awful bottle-tops. . . .

Several days later Niccolo stood on the palace landing
and gazed, as habitually he did, through the tall windows
at the beloved garden rising before him. The palace was
quiet, hardly a soul had come to visit it that day—still the
heat-wave persisted—and over the great halls and galleries
there weighed a ponderous, lifeless calm. Everything
around him was of the past, dead. Furniture, draperies,
and the reproachful figures of people in great paintings
made no movement. Such an impassive stance emphasized
the small noise of distant feet shuffling, of the single voice
of a visitor intoning upon a picture far along the gallery—
the presence of all those silent old things, and the arid
daylight which immobilized them, reflected and resounded
such contemporary life with the force of real echo.
Although Niccolo, as custodian, knew the worth of these
things, and often marvelled at their spirit—he was ma-
terially imprisoned by them. Sometimes he hated his job,
not as work but as a prison—and felt all the force of the

great wish to escape. Inside, the only relief to his eyes was the hall of entrance, where postcards and turnstiles and printed regulations brought a man down to everyday life. But the only true escape lay outside, with the garden, the grass, the enticing dark alleys of foliage—all those things that a deep and ancient instinct was denied.

Suddenly, like a cat that sees another through a window, his head jerked alertly to one side. He stared hard—beyond the courtyard, the fountain, the obelisk to that circular stone amphitheatre set above. On a terrace of urns and statues, against the dark oak-leaves, two figures stood. They were talking—it seemed with secrecy. They stood so nearly behind a statue that they might have thought themselves hidden by it. The larger figure was bent down whispering to the other, demonstrating with his hand. The other looked up and listened, patient. Ippolito! And one of those same ragged boys!

It was plain conspiracy—Niccolo was instantly on guard. That boy would never have been in the garden without Ippolito asking him there. And quickly the probabilities occurred to him. Although on that other afternoon the boys had finally escaped, nevertheless he remembered how he had found them first in Ippolito's district, near his home. Without a doubt Ippolito could have found them again. Instantly he thought—a witness to take to the directors! And then he thought—my pension.

On that other afternoon the episode of the boys and the bottle-tops had come to no climax, it had dwindled to a stop. As children will, the boys had got tired of fighting. They had returned to picking up what bottle-stoppers they could. Ippolito too in his muddled rage kept on flinging them out on to the gravel. So that soon few bottle-stoppers were left. The boys' sacks bulged full enough, Niccolo had emptied his long ago—he could throw no more in; and for his part the heat and a sore head from the previous night were beginning to tell—and he knew he had absented himself too long from his duties. Thus, while Ippolito and the boys were still dragging about in the mud for those declining stoppers, he had turned and, unnoticed, left.

The boys, their sacks full, had suddenly jumped from the pond and scuttled away into the cover of the trees. The nurse had turned all her wrath on the paddling Ippolito, accusing him against all his protestation of causing the trouble. This, to the outraged gardener, had been the most cruel stroke of all. He had subsided into a white temper—trembling at such injustice, and had watched in silence the nurse, his only witness, depart an enemy. He needed a witness badly. He had hobbled then over to the girl who had been asleep, and who was now lying with her head propped on an arm. He had implored her sympathy, pleaded with her to accompany him down to the office. But she with sleep still in her eyes—she must only then have woken up, and disclaimed any knowledge at all of the affair. Injustice had burst in Ippolito. He had thundered:

"Then pull your skirt down!"

This she did instantly and angrily. Her eye had caught his feet:

"And you—you put your boots on."

The next day Ippolito had approached his enemy with many threats. He accused him definitively of assault on the order of the Boboli, and stated his intention of bringing the affair immediately in front of the authorities. Niccolo had replied craftily, pretending fear and cursing himself for not having secured a witness—at which Ippolito, off his guard, had roared that neither had he himself a witness. Niccolo had then laughed and observed, with meaning, that it would be one word against the other. Ippolito knew he was defeated, the other would deny every word. The interview before the director could only result in a rising quarrel, it would look no more than that irresponsible behaviour was abroad, quarrels between the employees, lack of order—and that might mean dismissal for both of them. Thus, both knew, the question of witnesses became of absolute importance. And thus, seeing Ippolito now talking with the boy, Niccolo grew afraid.

Was the boy to be a witness? Could a boy be a witness? Moving to the side of the window, so that he too was partly hidden, Niccolo thought not. But could one be sure? Something, at least, was brewing. And then abruptly Niccolo held his breath—the worst, the most decisive had occurred. Now there was no question but of trouble. Ippolito had reached in his pocket and handed the boy a note of money. Money was scarce, money never passed without a serious object, and the more serious for Ippolito, who had won no lottery. And now the old keeper was handing the boy an object, a box, a parcel—it was difficult to see. Niccolo pressed his face against the window-pane to see—but suddenly they both vanished into the oak-hedge.

Some minutes later Niccolo turned and walked across the landing towards the stairway and the entrance hall. He was just in time to see the turnstile propel into the palace that small figure of the ragged boy. He began to run down the staircase—he would have shouted had the sanctity of those tall ceilings allowed. The boy must be stopped at all costs. He ran on, signing to the doorkeepers with raised arms. But they were greeting Ippolito who had just arrived and was entering too—though separately from the small boy.

"Giuglio, Luigi! That boy—that boy——"

They turned astonished. Niccolo! Red in the face! Puffing, blowing, waving his hands!

"That boy must not come in. I know him. Ragamuffin! Criminal! He'll break things, steal—quick!"

"What? Eh? But the boy has paid. . . he has shoes . . . he's old enough——"

"He has not shoes."

"Look there, he has."

"Then he has stolen them. He must not enter, I forbid it, I am guardian——"

"In that case, you're paid to see he does not steal; it's for you to watch him. As far as we are concerned——"

"And this old fool knows him too. Ippolito, what is this boy doing here?"

"Boy? Boy? I don't know any boy."

"Mother of God!"

"In any case, what boy? Where is there a boy?"

Niccolo looked round. The boy had already vanished. Panic started in his old frame, he swore at Ippolito, and hobbled off as fast as he could over the polished floor. He had no idea which way the boy had gone. He took the first turning at random. Through the long gallery he shuffled, looking behind every corner, into every recess— then stopped, looked back. Ippolito was making for the stairway. He paused, then purposely waited. Where Ippolito went, the boy was sure to be. He walked back slowly, judging the time when Ippolito would have reached the top of the stairs. He would follow quietly, catch them unawares; his old scarred hands grasped and spread like claws as he thought of that boy's shirt collar.

He peered round the corner and up the staircase—no sign of Ippolito. He must have reached the landing and disappeared. Swiftly, silently, breathing heavily with

these unaccustomed exertions, Niccolo followed up the
stairs. He reached the top, took a look along the gallery.
But he did not have to look far—there were Ippolito and
the boy, just inside the portal, only a few metres off, waiting. With a great grunt, swelling majestically, Niccolo
went forward. The boy simply stood there, his patient
angel's face waiting, his eyes on Niccolo's great hands
held out like claws to either side. Ippolito stood aside,
making no gesture, calmly stroking his long moustaches.

"Ah, my little fellow, now you come with me———"

And at the same time he grabbed forward. But his
hands closed on air. No boy. The boy had seemed to slide
back a full metre—and now remained waiting as before.
A most placid, magical escape—he had not ducked, or
side-stepped, or twisted away. Simply he had seemed to
recede, upright and staring. For a second Niccolo stood
astonished, his hands clawed together—perhaps he was
confused, perhaps out of breath, his old eyes were not
what they were.

He pounced forward again. Again his hands met on
air. Again the boy receded. This time Niccolo did not
wait, but instantly again lunged forward—and again the
boy mysteriously stood a metre off. And then, his eyes
staring hard at the small figure in front, a dreadful
sensation came over him—slowly, with viscose certainty,
he felt himself sliding backwards. He himself had made
no movement. An impalpable force was simply propelling
him back—or was the floor itself suddenly animate?
Looking at the boy in terror, he had the sensation of one
who stares at the quay from a ship slowly drawing off; or
as someone in a train watching through the window a
parallel carriage depart. Then suddenly he seemed to jerk
to a halt. Fearful, he looked to one side—but there still
stood Ippolito, and there to his right hand the wall where

he had first addressed the boy. He had not moved. It was the boy who had moved, gliding with magic backwards.

For a second there was silence, scarcely a movement. Panic caught at Niccolo's breath, held it—he was losing his reason. The boy simply waited, staring innocent with his appealing dark eyes, his small pure chin, his thin lips pressed in early sorrow. Only a slight movement from Ippolito, whose thick Roman frame shook within, whose eyes were watering, whose pink fat tresselated like hair beneath water—Ippolito containing the eddies of just governable laughter. And the old faun in his peaked cap crouched breathless, his upward-cast eyes fixed beneath their lids on the first magic in all his life that he had seen.

No visitors interrupted them. Again it was the hot afternoon, the great pause. Across the Arno, Florence slept—unconcerned in her austere walls with the minor antics of her people. Cities brood over their inhabitants with human, almost tender, concern; but it is a concern for all, not for one or two or three. As for centuries of summers, the graceless hard Duomo rose above its striped flanks. About it the lion-coloured streets bent their quietly violent ways. The great eaves hung overhead heavy as the heat, the windowless walls of prison-mansions stood firm and cheerless. The Arno flowed broadly, trying to lend softness to the gritty buff town—so did a few slender arcades; but they were stifled by the stuffed streets, the cruel Palazzo Vecchio and its museum square of dead statues, the hot torn horse-cabs piled with straw the whole dust-drunk torture of too-heavy streets towering and always about to fall, to crush, to smother. But in spite of such a stifling weight, such a dull monotonous colour, Florence remained a city, and so—in a grave, comprehending manner—maternal. But for private tragedy no city stirs—only perhaps, like some immense impassive beast, listens inwardly for a moment wondering where over all its great hide the tic has bitten.

Its brood was too great, that movement over in the Pitti was never really felt. Yet to Niccolo it was the whole world—a tremendous world of himself, the gliding-back boy, the dangerously lengthening floor, the height of the great ceiling ; for of that height and those lonely shadows far above he became unusually aware, they played a cathedral monotone over his moment of awe. Then in the next second he felt how much Ippolito was silently laughing, his native suspicion raced back, and with it his eyes opened wide and saw everything clearly. The angel knew this at once. He skidded round, and pressing forward on his magic feet slid off. There were wheels on his feet. With a sharp cry Niccolo was off after him at a hobbling run.

Roller skates are not common in Italy. The poorer streets are cobbled, though elsewhere, on the fine paving in piazza and terrace, there must extend smoother and more unique opportunities than in any other land. The floors of the Pitti Palace stretch polished, hard, endless. The grand corridor of rooms, each broad opening in perspective smaller than the last, gives the illusion of mirrors; but to the roller-skater blissfully they are not mirrors, but good rooms each with a polished floor— one could race down that central broad gallery at breath-taking speed, or curve in and out of the rooms slaloming like a skier, disappearing for a second behind a wall only to appear the next moment blinding obliquely across to another. One could disappear for whole minutes unknown in one room, intent on one's furious circle! Or, at will, one could traverse in precipitous run the entire length of the gallery, whistling through aperture after aperture like

an express beneath bridges, dizzying bridges that appear
and are gone like the shadows of birds, until, with a
mighty twist at the end, one shot out a foot and went
skidding round into other corridors avoiding the final
wall with hair's-breadth skill.

All this the boy knew—he knew exactly all he could do.
But he avoided the straight run—he wanted to keep near
Niccolo. And this he did with every device in his nimble
legs. No more an angel, his face had grown hot and eager.
And Niccolo had ceased at all to be a keeper—his features
were arched with lust—lust to capture, now the satyr on
the chase.

Against the boy he had no chance. His old feet not
cloven but weighted with boots and the rheumy years; his
bones all over slow; his blood running high; his breath
short ; his temper and sense whipped wild and bloodshot
as his eyes. What hope against those little wheels, the
young feet moving like fast boats, wedging in and out,
spreading and clicking together, shooting off at unthought
angles, swerving and darting and laughing at the awkward
stumbling old faun always just out of reach? Years of
duty—and that most tearful anger at injustice—kept old
Niccolo hobbling and sliding and plodding on, arms outstretched like a blind man. Only his face remained set,
cast and malicious—all the rest of him in its clumsy
black coat jerked and fluttered; yet that set face with its
long bones and its beaked nose became finally more piti-
ful than his body—its eyes slanted the terror of a trapped
beast. And Niccolo was an animal—for years he had
watched gardens that had curiously stirred him; for years
the dead palace floors had leadened his feet, longing for
the spring of earth, the pastures of his youth, the scent of
older and vaguer instincts for the grove and glade. Now
finally the palace had got him. The great walls looked

down on him limed by their treacherous floor... All
things remained quiet, a massive quiet of dust—only the
little whirring wheels and those two boots lurching. But
the wheels whirred so metal a noise that they too sounded
part of the silence—so that sometimes it seemed the old
faun battered about alone and mad among the vast empty
halls.

At length the boy grew tired. Abruptly he took to his
heels on the long straight run down a central passage, no
more appearing and vanishing between walls and pictures
and cases and furniture, but now a suddenly swift figure
speeding to its own diminution down the vast perspective, dwindling to a speck at its daylight bright end;
and leaving Niccolo blundering by himself, thinking the
boy still within distance—but now indeed alone and
thrashing with his hands at the quiet air, grunting at his
own stone echo. Until, whether from indignation at suddenly finding himself alone, or from sudden terror at
realizing himself solitary and inconceivable, or simply
from exhaustion, or from age, or from that great helpless
sense that might in any mind at some climactic moment
rise, from whatever of these agencies—in his confused
mind he could never have made clear—he collapsed; or
tripped by mistake or purpose on a thick carmine cord
and fell to the floor. He lay there, panting very slightly,
his eyes closed, and a ferocious animal curve—what
passes for a smile on the face of a faun-creature or a dying
shark—splitting his sculpted arched lips.

Ippolito had walked at leisure along the polished floor
after them. He had not attempted to keep pace—such
trouble would hardly have accorded with a scheme to
cause inconvenience. So he had walked at leisure, chuck-
ling with laughter at the success of his idea, and some-

times at a distance relishing the sight of the two figures, like smaller people in another world of mirrors, weaving to and fro at the end of the passage.

However, they disappeared. And Ippolito had by then had enough of his simple enjoyment. He began to walk faster. He had repaid the score, in any case matters had gone far enough; though the galleries were empty, it was stupid to risk undue trouble. And after all, such tricks on Niccolo were never devised quite ruthlessly, they were more in a manner of teasing—where the borderline between an obscure affection and malice cannot clearly be drawn. Ippolito decided that the time had come to reclaim the skates from that boy. They had to go back to the shop from which he had borrowed them.

Thus he quickened his walk to the end of the gallery, turned the corner—and there in a recessed room suddenly saw Niccolo lying still where he had fallen on the floor. His concern was instant—shocked, he raised his old colleague's head, listened for breath, propped him up comfortably, ran off for assistance.

Two days later Niccolo was conscious again. He began to renew his strength. A little later he was allowed home from the hospital. He lay in his own bed, and though it was plain he had suffered for his age a most severe shock, nevertheless there began a gentle slow recovery. Ippolito visited him every day. He brought whatever he could. He went to great pains to help in any way the unfortunate man. His remorse was evident, he regretted deeply the ill he had caused. And more than this, he discovered in himself a genuine tender affection for the other old man. Willingly Niccolo returned this. Everything was forgiven. It was as if the sudden shock had jolted them, the futility of such uneasy neighbourhood had been shown up—the envy and scorn resolved into a purer interest,

and in the face of misfortune they found the true friend-
ship that had lain beneath.

Then, as the weeks wore on and Niccolo grew very
much better, as he recovered his old strength and took a
more active interest in life, as his white face took on its
olive colour again and he took his first careful walks—
Ippolito found himself once or twice becoming short-
tempered with his friend. Resolutely he fought this back.
It was a very small irritation. But nevertheless it occurred
repeatedly; then more and more frequently. At last,
though afterwards they were both quick to apologize,
they broke into an open quarrel.

And Niccolo grew stronger and stronger.

STREET SONG

—

NAPLES lumped sprawling round its bay, a sunbaked leviathan. Its curve of winking ochre dozed rough and old and calm; but within the tegument a monstrous dark life bubbled and boiled, deep spawning veins pulsed and coursed with tidal effort. Vesuvius rose above, its summit blue and smokeless: it was the monster below that smoked. A yellow haze of smoke hung over the hot city: it shimmered, a mirage seen over the ancient sea that stretched out before it, a sea sparkling clean like chipped blue crystal.

It was to this city that one day there came that wise traveller, Jason. He came from the landward approach, in a chromium motor-bus. He came primed with energy, busy with guile, intent on conquering this new city. He considered himself, with satisfaction, to be a most efficient traveller; he 'knew his way around'; he felt that, with chameleon cunning, he could merge and mix unrecognizably with the people of whatever land he visited. He had his systems. By 'conquering a city' he meant that he would assimilate the city, explore it and know it, turn it inside out, and learn both its feeling and its inner secrets during a limited visit. He would retire 'knowing' the city. He had some suspicion that at such assault the cities smiled, opening themselves casually to inspection, revealing here a quality, there a vista, here a tendency, there a prospect. But cities were constructed of walls, walls had corners, and behind each lay something more— casually hidden. Also, the more that was known the more complicated that knowledge became; each pattern contained another pattern. Knowledge grew; but compounding upon itself shattered each stage of generality. However—Jason always approached with optimism, anticipating only success, certain of his strength. And in this case, even before Naples was reached, the battle was on.

He had come from Rome, and from his soft seat in the swift torpedone had noted with gratification that the Kingdom of the Two Sicilies seemed still to exist. Somewhere after Gaeta, and certainly by the time Capua was reached, the character of the villages and the towns had changed absolutely. This was not so much an architectural as a social change—for here one began driving from the Roman solidities into a land of disrepair, a land where poverty squatted slack-jawed on the streets, where the streets lay kerbless and littered, where plaster and brick had decayed not in patches but over whole alleys and squares, where carts were patched up with rope and all energy had to be expended on only first necessities, where dilapidation like a disease had eaten so fast that nothing anyone ever did hereafter could hope to begin ever to put it straight: one had entered King Bomba territory, land of the old tyrant and his rabid lazzaroni.

As they had entered the outskirts of Naples itself, this chaos of dust and ruin had grown to nightmare strength. But even before the city began, the tramline appeared with its dreadful symbolic direction. Many kilometres from the city proper it started, to travel then a perpetual track by the side of the road in a ruthless straight line towards the unseen city. Weeds had sprung up between the rails, grasses bowed as the metropolitan trams barged along isolated and dreamlike against their rustic background. Though of course such trams ran out of the towns elsewhere in Italy, here the scale of their journey and the straightness of that line heralded the huge proportion and the pitiless character of the ancient capital approached.

Then they passed an increasing impedimenta of mules and lumbering carts—and the broad dusty metropolis had engulfed them; it had seemed to spread itself out and take them at speed along the wandering wide alimentary roads into its turbulent maw. Such a yellow mist of dust, such a clamouring of people, such teeming stalls and booths and barrows, such a display of rags and washing and torn sheaths of paper—as though these were the city's panoply of white and grey flags put out fluttering everywhere from every window to address the traveller; it seemed too that the city had turned itself out of doors, everyone had tumbled out on to the pavements, leaving their decrepit houses empty. On into the centre where massive buildings began to rise among the struggling houses, buildings built of a stone darker than elsewhere, of a gloomy leaden grey under the sun, slab-grey of prisons and dark justice—past the great railway station, past martial angels astride growling black lions, straight down the last canyon of granite office buildings to the terminal sea. Here the torpedone stopped. Jason descended and, waiting for his luggage, took in the grand perspective.

It was not grand. It was ragged, immense, confusing. Before one arrives at a city as known as Naples, a preconceived picture has been built. Thus all his life Jason had loosely imagined the bay—as described for him by water-colours and optimist novels—as a grand clear sunlit crescent, capped by vast Vesuvius, containing the town neatly at its centre; somehow the town, an amorphous but neat huddle of balconied houses, had centred on one street leading downhill to a promenade. This street was also balconied, and had at its end the wine, the electric

bulbs, the leafy ceiling of a gay restaurant called Zi'
Teresa. So the neat crescent of the town had been divided
neatly by a neat street—all as compactly visible as a stage
set, though of course larger. There had been a patch of
fishing boats, one or two vines and many people singing.

But standing outside the bus office, at what was the
central hub of sunny Napoli, he was confronted with a
most unmanageable, shapeless vista. Not a square, but a
formless undulating patch of gardens and wide streets of
unwalkable proportion, with at one corner of the eye a
skein of dock fences and port offices, at the other a far
wall of sun-dried hotel and municipal buildings, and in
front not the sea but above several ragged palms a mound
capped by the grim, dark, cruelly towered fortress-palace
of the Angevins—the Castel Nuovo. Over this perspective trams rattled and lorries drove. One was bewildered,
one could not see which way to walk. But cities are never
as compact as their maps, there is always a long walk
ahead. Jason nodded his head wisely, muttered his 'we
shall see,' and grabbed his luggage handed down from the
bus-top.

Instantly a circle of faces formed round him, hands
grabbed his sleeve, others tried to wrest away his suitcase, peaked caps advertising hotels touched themselves
and bowed. Looking at no one, making certain not to
meet personally any eye—for at the least sign of weak-
ness, even a word, the efforts of these people would be re-
doubled—he made for the bus-office door. It was a
battle, a thrusting and pulling against hands and bodies.
'No' had no effect. And even then, as Jason achieved the
office door, a last figure presented itself—short, dark,
gold-toothed, agonized. From an impassioned mouth
there streamed an endless complaint. It was the bus
porter. Jason had given him nothing for handing down

his bag—a matter of lifting it, and passing it several feet downwards. But this was service. Cursing, Jason fumbled his free hand—it would have meant disaster to leave go of his heavy bag—in a pocketful of small notes. Sweating in the sunlight, he tried to select twenty lire. The man helped him and took forty. Jason hurried into the office. 'Ah well,' he excused himself, 'it was only sixpence.' In this he glossed over the erosive truth that a voyage may be shipwrecked by 'only sixpences.'

Inside the office—surprisingly clean and cool, faultless as an air terminal—he regained his assurance. *Now* he knew what to do. *Now* things would go according to *his* plan. He had calculated carefully a strict system of travel. Not for Jason the booking of hotels in advance, not for him the sheeplike recommendations of friends. Arrived anywhere, he went immediately to the luggage office and disencumbered himself. That done, the job was to move round the town throughout the day, walking, taking trams and buses, assimilating the geography and the feeling of the place against the blueprint of his pocket map. By the end of the day he would know roughly what the town had to offer. On the way he would have noticed several possible hotels of a character that he found interesting and at a price within his pocket. Towards the end of the afternoon he would return to one of these, book a room and collect his luggage. To fulfil such an exercise he always said: 'Make sure you arrive in the morning, early.' And: 'One day's hard work, and you know where you are.'

So disembarrassed of his luggage, he came on to the pavement again—his feet after the bus feeling logged as a landed sailor's. Now things would pass more slowly. Instinctively he turned back the way he had come. He walked briskly round the corner and up the Via Depretis.

But after a minute he stopped—the arterial avenue looked broader and much longer than before. He excused himself—pleading that the grey ranks of office buildings promised nothing. He turned tail. He came again to the bus office—and stood there wondering. A tout disengaged himself from the wall. This decided Jason, and he was off walking over the straggling gardens to where the distant municipal buildings stood livid pink in the sun. The sun was hot—walking from the shade it hit on to the head with physical force, with the touch of hot iron. He knew from his map that nearby in that direction lay the old port, the romantic water of Zi' Teresa. Nearby; but the map gave no idea of the hard pavements, of the dusty air, of the sunglare, of the size of the buildings to be passed. Thus Jason strode along a course directed to the sea, the sea hidden by the great castle mound. Round by the Piazza del Plebescito, cold and pallid; past the enormous pink-and-grey Palazzo Reale, vast barracks of heavy kings; a brief glimpse of the sea from the high promenade, then the turn into the street called Santa Lucia—from here brief glances up dark alleys that breathed of refuse and stiletto, of the brawling lazzaroni; at last out on to the promenade opposite the old port, with the grim Castello d'Ovo at the end of the mole. But here was no singing life of green jalousie and balcony, no fantasia of straw-hat and neapolitan pink; instead, a solid urban promenade, faced with a line of large hotels. The sea below looked scrappy, a mess of old port-work and breakwater, of bathing establishment and outbuilding— no seductive beach here; Naples seemed finally to reveal itself, a monster city as heavy as Manchester. Away to the north lay the curve of what looked like another land, the resident perspective of Posillipo; back south the smoking port and Vesuvius hulking beyond; ahead indeed the sea—but the sea only attained its sapphiric calm splendour far away, out towards the horizon and the hazed mysteries of Capri and Ischia.

Jason turned away disappointed. But then, as he walked upwards into the narrower streets, he met the old town, and there he was transported into Naples of the street song; but a street song more violent than any he had hitherto imagined.

In the first place, there was no connection with the sea. You could not see it, nor smell it, nor feel it—unless a few indigenous fish on a restaurant menu could be counted. Certainly there were sailors about, Neapolitan fishermen and sailors off the harboured ships—but these were not sailors rolling off the quayside, they were dusty sailors caught up in a town, no salt clung to these. Secondly the incidence of balcony and green-painted blind, of paper flowers and all the gaudy gimcrack flourish of the century's turn—this proved stronger than he had imagined. It occurred in patches, yet pervaded the whole with its papery nostalgic charm. And in texture it went farther than he had imagined—there was almost a japanoiserie abroad. Thirdly, these streets teemed with a voluble, vigorous, violent ant-hill life of rags and song and struggle difficult to believe—something more arabic or eastern than Italian. And fourthly—the dirt. The ubiquitous dirt. The smears and stains and piles and promontories of dirt: the calligraphic effect, almost of camouflage, that this tattering of refuse wrote over everything. Jason stopped—astounded. He backed against a shop window and tried to assess what he saw, to select from such a gushing turbulence some outline that could be remembered.

He explained it thus to himself. Really, he had stopped for two other reasons. He could not decide whether this

street or the next or the next was the one he should select
—he was always frightened of missing something, often
he walked half-way up a street and then turned back. And
secondly—and this was perhaps the most forceful argument—the street looked dangerous, it was filled with dark-
eyed people who looked as energetic as they were poor,
who seemed with their incessant cries and wild argument
and swift movement to be caught up in a struggle to the
death for money. Thus both greed and fear, insidious
despoilers of the lonely traveller, prompted him to look
for refuge and continue his observations from there. But
in such streets there were no café tables, the streets were
too narrow, cafés had not been thought of when these
tortuous houses were built. Across the road a doorless
cavern showed murkily its barrelled, wine-stocked in-
terior: too dark. He happened then to glance behind
him—the very window on which he leant covered an ice
and coffee bar. He went inside and stood at the counter
near the door.

Jason stood near the door to see outside; he stood up
at the counter because he knew it was cheaper—rather
less to save money than because he knew about it. Any
other Englishman (he told himself) would have sat down
and taken for granted that things cost twenty per cent.
more than they did. Although he would have liked a
brandy, he decided to order coffee: important to keep the
brain clear this first day—and besides the Italians all
drank coffee, it was the cheap drink, it was the thing. So
when the barman leant over to him, he produced one of
his carefully prepared speeches. These were seldom
grammatically correct, but he delivered them with a
faultless accent. He had a very rough knowledge of
Italian; it was rough because he had spent too much time
practising his accent. His instinctive ear welcomed the

strange sound; but above all he liked to dramatize himself; and moreover he had a horror of sounding ridiculous or inferior—so that he learned always to *appear* to speak a language perfectly. More imagination would have told him that a foreign accent can be charming, and usually is—whereas a stumbling and stuttering tries the patience of the listener. Thus only the prepared phrases came out easily; but no more than these. However there was a singular exception—he achieved always a magical fluency when he was drunk. This should have taught him long before that self-assurance is the secret of speaking any foreign language. But he was afraid of being laughed at, of failure.

He said to the waiter: "Piacere, caffe espresso." (That was fine, he knew even the technical kind of coffee.)

The waiter said: "Con zucker?"

"Si, grazie."

The interchange was perfect; Jason adjusted himself with pleasure from an awkwardly nonchalant position with his arm on the counter to a less conscious stance on his two true Italian feet. But just as the sweet black coffee came steaming towards his hand, the barman's face again obtruded. This time its mouth opened, and there issued a stream of fluid Italian that sounded blankly to his ear as one endless serpentine word. He stood there speechless. The silence stammered. It hung like empty lead. He could only think wildly that probably the man was praising the coffee, or the weather, or stating some politic of the moment. Agreement was the only course. So, smiling wisely, frowning as man to man, he nodded and intoned: "Si, si."

Another silence. The man stared at him unmoved, open-eyed. And then the sentence started again, but this time emphatically, rising in tone. Then suddenly it stopped, the man gave a laugh and broke into easy English. A man was coming to deliver the cakes and would he please move a little up the counter?

Jason whispered: "Prego."

He turned to look at the street. Humiliating. He had lost the first round with this leviathan city. He became more alert, tightened his defences. Now with an acute eye he considered the street. What exactly was happening there?

In the first place, life was lived at several levels. On each of the four tiers of balconies, between long swathes of washing hung out on poles, there moved a plane of life; heads poked from the windows and called to the street, other heads poked upwards and talked with others on the balconies above. Dark-eyed women sewed, washed, arranged potted flowers on their balconies and just within their cooler rooms. A radio blared from one, a canary sang in another, from another someone clattering pans in a kitchen gave free and joyful voice to a Verdi aria—it was astounding how all Italians seemed to know by heart the scores and lyrics of a dozen operas. Then there was the lowest, the street level, darkly shaded from the blue furnace far removed above. Here some fifty or sixty Neapolitans must have moved within the few square yards of his viewpoint. Some passed straight by, others obliquely from shop-door to shop-door, others stood and talked in the street's centre, others bent over their work or cried their wares from the shop-doors. The doors were cavernous, like the openings to coach-houses. Opposite stood the wine shop, dispensing darkly its stale wooden wine-smells. Next, three men blackened with grit and oil hammered and twisted at wheels and mudguards, a yellow blowlamp candled a mass of dead machines that rose like stacked treasure behind them. The next cavern poured fruit and vegetables out over the street—yellow and green pimentoes, zeppelin pumpkins, a horde of scarlet dwarf tomatoes, frog-green grapes dribbling and spawning everywhere: the fruit looked as if it was pouring, torrentially, into the street—pavement and baskets and paper were smeared and sodden with crushed juice and wasp-bitten rind. On the other side of the wine-cave, a clothier's—its packed empty suits and uniforms drooped to either side of the doorway like the residue of a mass hanging; in the doorway, trestles with more clothes— ancient dress uniforms of tramway and army, yellowing grey cloth-bales, bright new overalls—and wedged glassily among these an oleograph of Vittore Emanuele II and two or three, illuminated, of the Virgin. Next door lay the only quiet place, a cavern studded like a cemetery with china bowls and lavatory pans; no one jostled in this place, its only occupant was a small sad man, grey in the half-light, who squatted waiting on one lavatory—it was the only one with the seat down. And then, since these cluttered precincts did not quite fill the crowded narrow prospect, each shop had stationed in front of it street-sellers with tables on their laps and tubs at their sides, sellers of ices and sweets and fruits and cigarettes and hot pancakes and cheese and lotteries and hairpins and sacred effigies and socks. Thus, another curtain of movement added to the stew, for what altogether this could mostly be felt as was a kitchen, a hot broiling kitchen of food and drink to stuff in the mouth, hash of tomatoes and nougat and grapes all bound with a rubbery cream of warm mozzarella, condimented with hot black cycle-oil and a pepper of song.

He began to walk again, zigzagging with foreign courtesy through the crowd, going deeper into the warm cavernous streets uphill: then suddenly debouched into a

wider road. Pavements had been laid, but they had
crumbled and many blocks were missing Again the sun
struck; Jason pressed himself on, glanced efficiently over
every building as he passed, puzzled that he had seen no
hotel yet to his taste—he had imagined some green-
balconied retreat smothered in bougainvillea, cool with
courtyards, perhaps a fountain—yet telling himself that
the day was still young. But it was already midday. The
sun beat down its heavy blue, hardening all it touched
with a metallic, golden radiance.

Many Neapolitans turned and watched Jason as he
threaded his careful way through the crowds. Some hurried on, but others swivelled straight at him—demanding
him to buy cigarettes, fountain-pens, tortoiseshell boxes,
and, in the case of some of the small boys, their sisters.
All these received a predestined 'no'—sometimes muttered, sometimes angry, sometimes even shouted, for
Jason was most sure of his negative when walking at
some speed. He told himself firmly that on no account
would he be 'done' by these people so celebrated for their
skill. But what made him really more angry was that he
should be spotted at all—and addressed so very often in
English or French.

One of Jason's most confirmed conceits grew from a
belief that he could pass unnoticed as a native citizen. For
instance, he never set out for Paris without first placing
on his legs black-and-grey striped trousers and on his feet
brown shoes; above these he would wear a dark-blue jacket
of suiting, a bow tie, a grey trilby hat placed very straight.
Thus he became overnight a Frenchman of ordinary
family: except to the Frenchman, who noticed instantly
his English carriage, the cut of his clothes, and most
probably an English paper he had forgotten to hide. And
now in Naples he wore a white jacket, a straw hat, in-

different trousers of thin material and sandals. He had chosen with satisfaction a Calabrian type of classic sandal, relegating others bought near Genoa to his suitcase. 'The Tyrrhenian, no more the Ligurian,' he breathed. He would not have been wrong a few miles farther down the coast. But naked feet with their single toe-string were never meant for the dust and melon-rind of Naples, nor for the brownish lake of urine that spread out from a street-lavatory he was at that moment passing. It was the same with other fancies—all were a little out of context. A white coat—but too white, and of English cut: those milling southerners, who seemed to wear such endlessly various clothes, would recognize in the first instant some reserved peculiarity of English tailoring. His hat worn on the nordic back of his head, not down across the eyes against the southern sunshine; moreover, it was dented, and that was not Neapolitan. He was far too white and clean. Much white may be seen among the elegancies of Rome and Venice, but the poverty of Naples has drowned all clear colours—and most certainly white. Rags, rags that exposed lengths of bare arm and thigh, walked everywhere; and only few of the unragged wore thin clothes, for they wore the same winter and summer. Colours had faded and greyed with dirt. Jason had noticed this—it was sadly obvious—but had naturally excluded himself. He could hardly have hoped, though he did, to pass for less than a man asking aloud to be accosted.

Now he walked on yet farther—past a fish-seller with trays of fine fat tunny-fish and long squids like rubber surgical devices with soapy tails, past a brightly streamered tavern announcing the Piedegrotta, past a dwarf shouting lottery tickets, past a donkey spruce in silver and red-tasselled Sicilian harness, past an enormous armoured-looking tram, past a man singing, past a

woman so tired one felt she would never cry again—
past the end of these older streets and out from the chaos
of the poor into the cacophony of rich and poor mixed. Out
again into that first part of larger buildings where a
sudden glass-plated shop showed rich optical instruments,
where the enormous rustications of a palace showed this
as a heavyweight place, a monster among ports, a place as
tasteless in one of its great bombastic buildings as it was
charming in some delicate next. The tops of the insides
of Jason's legs began to sting. It was the old trouble. He
was chafed. The sweating heat and this walking had made
him so sore he would be in pain for the next day.

Ordinarily he could not easily decide to sit down at any
particular café—he always imagined a better one round
the corner, and thus often went thirsty. But now the hot
raw stinging decided him, he looked round, and by a
singular stroke of luck saw opposite a café with tables in
the street. It was indeed luck—he had seen no other open-
air café yet. This one was surrounded by a shallow fence
of dark-green creeper. He went in and sat down. To the
right rose the immense barracks of the Palazzo Reale;
to his left the opening to the Umberto Gallery, its curved
steps alive with shoeblacks; somewhere modestly ahead
the San Carlo Opera House retreated in grimy shadow.
Between these three landmarks the traffic rushed and
rattled and swerved and braked endlessly; trams, lorries,
carts, filo-buses, cars, motor-cycles gave off dark clouds
of bad petrol and tore up the dust. Jason saw why there
were few open-air cafés.

This time he ordered from the smiling waiter a glass
of wine. The waiter looked upset. A glass of wine—
surely a bottle? Then—if that must be so—a bottle of
Orvieto? When Jason, who knew Orvieto was expensive,
repeated that he wanted a glass of ordinary wine, the

waiter explained that this could be obtained only in a wine tavern, not in a café. Here were only beer, lemonade, orangeade, coffee ... and suddenly at the word 'orangeade' the back of Jason's mouth itched dryly for bubbles, for iced chemical sweet bubbles. The sun and the dust drove in hotly. He ordered an orangeade, beside himself, and in English. The waiter, who must have been a thoughtful man, had made his explanations so far in slow pidgin-Italian. Now he said: "Yessir, orangeade" in English, and bustled away. Jason smiled to himself. Having taken a decision and selected a café, he could afford to laugh at a little defeat of this kind.

When the waiter came back, he asked where the restaurant called Zi' Teresa was. The waiter crumpled up his face in astonishment. Zi' Teresa? Teresa? He had no idea.

But for once Jason grew definite, and most firmly said he did not believe any Neapolitan living on this side of the town could not know such a world-celebrated place. For once, also, he was right. The waiter understood such firmness, his face uncrumpled and smiled. Zi' Teresa? Naturally he knew Zi' Teresa. It was at Santa Lucia, down by the water. But ... it was very expensive, one had to pay much money, many lire, not like here. And pursing his lips and shaking his head like a nurse warning her charge against the fearful gipsies, he was off. Jason felt disappointed. Here as usual was one of the plums of the city elevated above his pocket by the usual inflation.

A man sitting at a nearby table had been watching him for some time. Jason had felt the man's head turning round at him several times. Now left alone without the waiter, he took a quick glance, pretending to look over the man's head. He turned quickly back to his orangeade—the man had been reading an English paper; more, he had held this paper's headlines purposely towards Jason—obviously to introduce himself. A middle-aged man, pleasant-looking, inconspicuous except for what seemed that roving, purposeful eye; Italian eyes roved, but they kept on roving, they never held one like English eyes. One expected from an Italian eye the approbatory: 'Are you going to be any use to me, will you like me?' From an English eye you received a harder approbation, rapidly souring to disapproval, that said: 'You are not like me. You are different in this way, in that way. You belong to such and such a type of people. I don't like you.'

But strangely—there are so many exceptions to the rule—the man's face was peering above Jason's orange-ade, smiling and excusing himself. Here was no diffident Englishman.

"Excuse me, I could not help overhearing what you said. I'm English, too. Heard the waiter tell you Zi' Teresa's expensive. Absolute nonsense, of course, not much dearer than anywhere else, fellow only wanted you never to go anywhere else but here."

Jason thanked him, and warming despite himself to the sound of an English voice, asked him if he would care to have a drink? The man sat down and said he had only been in Naples two days. After he had ordered, in blatant English, a brandy and water, Jason asked him:

"And how do you find Naples?"

"What do you think? Filthy hole. Filthy dirty. See Naples and die, eh? —I'd say—smell Naples and——"

Jason knew what was coming, and cut in before the final pain, surging suddenly in defence of Naples:

"Oh, come. There's more to it than that. Its history is fascinating, and in all this—chaos—there's a tre-mendous—charm——"

These words he said slowly, realizing that beyond his

first impulse to argue he felt genuinely this charm. He had not noticed that before. The man muttered again about the dirt, but Jason again interrupted him:

"Think, for instance, of our English delight in Neapolitan Street Songs. Certainly, they exist. But what do you really hear when you listen to the people singing for themselves? Not 'Santa Lucia,' not 'O Sole Mio,' but music straight from that combination of brain and stomach called not the heart but the soul—they sing the music of Arabs. Like southern Spaniards, who tear their throats softly with the rise and fall of Flamenco airs. Strong blood from Africa—look at them—they *are* Arabs."

Jason stopped suddenly as he waved his hand at the tumultuous passing in front of him, as he saw the startled blue eyes of the man, as he looked then down with misgiving at his innocent orangeade. He said:

"I'd better have a brandy."

The other man was looking at him startled:

"Good Lord, you ought to meet Dale."

"Dale?"

"As a matter of fact, he's coming along in a few minutes."

"Dale?"

"You'd like him. Knows a lot about this place. Poetic chap, like yourself. Personally, of course, I don't get it— look at that there——"

He waved his hand at a group that had suddenly gathered gesticulating round some sort of argument. Three or four men, shabbily and raggedly dressed, flashed dark eyes, gold teeth, word-weaving hands at each other; already a woman with watering red eyes and a white ill child was holding out her hand to them; two small boys, shoeless and thin, wisps of boys, but brown and active, had dived already between their shoes and were scrabbling for a cigarette end that one of the ragged men, miraculously, had been smoking. Within a minute all this was over, everyone had gone elsewhere, only a piece of pinkish paper fluttered on the smeared, sunbaked pavement where they had stood—and even this piece of paper moved on to join others of its kind.

Jason said:

"Yes, how could it be charming? Poverty, ill-nourished children, everyone scrambling and cutting each other's throats for the scraps of life, the cigarette butts? I suppose the answer is that it isn't—but sometimes feels so. It's something to do with vigour, interest in life. Suppose, for instance, you are watching a film—and a character walks past a barrow and pinches an apple. If his face expresses only the thin lips of hunger, you are filled with pity; if his face looks mean and shifty, you are shocked and condemn; if he uses some amusing sleight of hand and brightens inwardly with satisfaction, you laugh and wish the fellow well. All the same action, all prompted by need of the apple, the same economic need. Just so, there is this energy and lack of fear, this vigour in the sun which appeals to us in the Neapolitan scrum: no apathy, no defeat, you never see one of them bored. And of course they live under the sun—which they themselves consciously love, though it is always with them. They're proud of their sun. And again there's another matter—the continuity of living, something in the ground perhaps where people have milled and struggled for so many thousands of years—I don't know. Nor do I know why there seems to be an appeal in their two-faced character of heartlessness and generous love."

"Yes, but——"

"But you're right, it's perfectly awful. Only sometimes it doesn't seem quite so bad. However——"

And Jason talked on, expanding his theme, changing
to another, riding on the desire that always rose in him
abroad to give local information wherever he was. He
liked to tell people all about it. This attentive fellow-
countryman with the startled blue eyes proved a fine
audience. The sun beat down fiercely. Jason sat in the
shade to be more sensible, more Italian. In his bedroom he
would sit for hours in the sun, continually shifting his
chair to catch the rays as they moved relentlessly across
the room. But not in public. The brandy—and they had
ordered more—went down comfortably. More than ever
the Italians seemed to smile.

Then Dale arrived. A thin, sharp-looking man with
spectacles and an amused mouth. He ordered an Italian
aperitif and listened for a moment to Jason finishing:

"Why do they sing, why do they charm?"

"Parthenope, I suppose."

"Parthenope?"

"The siren," Dale said. "The one cast up on the bay
here, and after whom the place was first named."

"Oh—I didn't know."

"She and her sisters used to sit on a rock quite nearby.
Sang and charmed everyone. But poor Parthenope fell in
love with a man and was cast ashore. As you know, the
coast abounds with talk of them. In other forms the myth
exists to this day. Of course that was long before Palæopolis——"

"Eh?"

"Palæopolis and Neapolis, the first recorded cities,
founded from Cumæ, Greek in character of course.
Whether or not Æneas *did* actually land here can't be
decided—but I like to think it, don't you? Same sun,
same glittering sea—it feels remarkably, remarkably
ancient, remarkably Greek still too. More than a thou-

173

sand years after the Romans won that great battle——"

"Battle?"

"The battle of Mount Vesuvius. Three hundred and forty before, I think."

And on the man went. Jason sat deflating, deflated. How he wished he had looked up a bit about this ancient stuff, how he wished he could feel it as Dale could! But without the magic words, without the book written and solid before him, with Dale's personality drowning what he said . . . it was difficult. He gazed moodily at a passing soldier, immensely upholstered with leather cartridge-belts and black moustaches deadly against his khaki. Suddenly something struck him, and he made a last attempt.

"A thing that strikes me is the extreme to which Naples goes. The thoroughness of it all. Look at that street—how does it look so much more shabby than the shabby streets of other towns, towns also with leprous walls, poverty, blind windows? See—it's the road between . . . the texture is everywhere the same, the road itself is as mottled as the walls. Other towns have clean, or nearly clean streets —that act like clean stages to the blown back-drop. But here an impious camouflage covers the whole, no relief whatsoever, everything you see is streaked and mottled, the walls with the age of years, the street with its wet smears and refuse—the age of a day. And the sun's clear light shows every mark."

"I wonder," said Dale, "how it was in the time of the Aragonese. What did Alfonso see of it?"

Then they were among the Aragonese, the Habsburgs, the Bourbons. They went backwards through the Ange-vins, the Normans. Then they went to lunch. Jason was silenced absolutely. Nor could he remember much of what was being said. And during lunch two matters came to

disturb him. The first concerned food. To have a practical
eating knowledge of all national dishes and ways of cook-
ing was one of Jason's small conceits; it afforded cover
in the battle with waiters, it was worldly stuff to repeat at
home. But he was cursed with a good appetite—an in-
herited peasant hunger learnt at the tables of a boarding
school and of a needlessly economic middle-class home.
So that whenever he sat down to a meal, lust for survival
anxiously murmured that this might be his last. His
appetite rose, he felt that at all costs (except that to his
pocket) he must eat a lot. Thus he read with slow care
through entire menus, considering the romantic possibili-
ties of a dozen strange dishes, but with an inward terror
that though tempting to the palate they might not satisfy
his hunger. There might not be enough on the plate!
So, after tempting himself a dozen times with strange
palatal adventures, more often than not he decided to
play safe. This was one of those days. He ordered
spaghetti with tomato sauce and afterwards a beef stew.
Spaghetti would be filling, there was always more meat
in a stew.

When the spaghetti arrived, he was not exactly wrong
—plenty of spaghetti but with its dull tomato sauce that
he might have eaten anywhere in Italian London. Dale,
however, had ordered a pasta marinata, which proved to
be an equally high pile of spaghetti but studded with crisp
currants of fresh fried shell-fish; and the other man was
brought an omelet, a large omelet of pale yellow, whose
every mouthful dripped succulent strings of cream cheese.
Much worse was to follow. Jason's stew proved a dribbling small business, the Italians not being much interested in such dishes. But Dale was given a plate over-
flowing with golden mixed fried fish—fat thumb-size
prawns, loops of soft cuttle-fish, queer long-nosed fish

that when opened revealed against their white flesh bright viridian bones! And on the other's plate brown medallions of veal glistened with dark marsala!

Munching through this, and through a dessert of fine grapes and peaches, Dale gave generously of the history of Naples.   On and on he went:

". . . then the dark Aragonese Ferrante had a peculiarity strange even for a quattrocento despot—he liked to keep near to him embalmed in their customary clothes the dead bodies of his enemies. This, the successor to Alfonso the Great, who on military expeditions insisted that the classics be read to him and whose obsession with antiquity was such that he rode into Naples triumphant in a gilded chariot——"

Listening vaguely to such as this, Jason was looking towards the door and window where a patch of sunlight showed. Above the window curtain, the top balcony of a house and a wedge of blue sky, distant blue sky; past the doorway people passed with the rustle of life. How exciting suddenly this sunlight, seen through prison bars, proved! How much more to be treasured than the remote monologue of past centuries! What adventures, adventures immediately, the sunlight promised! How one wanted to escape—how very often the doors of restaurants had promised escape!

The bill was brought. It was agreed to share it. It was one of Jason's systematic ideals to read thoroughly each item scribbled by the waiter, and even to check the addition. It was important not to be cheated, it was vital to avoid the waiter's smile triumphing behind one's back as one left. But most often Jason lost courage; with the waiter's eye on him he merely pretended to check the bill—and was quick to finger in his pocket for money. This he now did, placing an enormous lire note on the plate. Instantly Dale whisked the bill away, frowning and shaking his head:

"Never, without checking it."

He read slowly and at leisure that long scribble of figures. His eyebrows went up and he called the waiter. Something was said in Italian. The waiter clutched his head with apology, took out a pencil and revised the price.

"Saved us a few hundred," Dale smiled.

At last they were out in the street.

"Well," said the first man—his name seemed to be Hislop, but he was the kind of man whose name is seldom mentioned, a 'you' man—"Well, that was very nice. I do hope we'll meet again. Are you going to the Piedigrotta?"

"I beg your pardon?"

"The Piedigrotta. To-night."

"Ah. Well—I'm not sure yet whether I can———"

"It'll be difficult for him to avoid it," Dale laughed; "but I'm not sure that our friend is unconfused ... the Piedigrotta is one of the most important festivals in the Neapolitan year, and one of the most lively in the world. To-night's the culminating night—fireworks on the grandest scale out on the bay, much dancing in the streets, not a little of the wine of high spirits. You'll see the people at their best. Better not miss it."

Jason could have killed him. But before he could even reply, Hislop was saying:

"Come along with us. We're meeting at Auntie's at seven."

At the same time, Dale took off his glasses. He looked far less dangerous, the glinting was gone, and his pale eyes looked weak and helpless. Jason said:

"It's very good of you. I'll try. I'm not sure whether I can get away. I'll try."

He had no one, of course, from whom to get away. He

had not even an hotel. But sincerely he wanted to avoid
these two, and at the same time to leave an impression
that his time was not unfilled, that he was no solitary
upon whom pity should be taken. At last they were gone,
and he was walking away fast in the opposite direction.
It was also the opposite direction to that in which he
wanted really to go. But the joy of being alone again, the
freedom for adventure! Why spend these valuable hours
with English people, one had plenty of time for that at
home! Now for more of the true Neapolitan life! The
moment had to be lived. After all, poor Dale . . dreaming
remote from the moment, dreaming of the past. Action!
He did not know then, as he was later told, that Dale had
already hired a carrozza to take him to his mistress's
house, a Pozzuolian lady with whom he spent many
pleasurable afternoons, and to whose house he had first
been invited purely on account of his unhungry, easy,
remote behaviour.

So Jason wished on, destroying his chances by wishing.
And suddenly found himself, like a homing-bird, by the
bus station again! At last he laughed at himself.

"Come, come, we must do better than this."

It had also flashed across him suddenly that 'Auntie's'
meant Zi' Teresa's.

However, he had no intention of going there. The
English had to be avoided. Now he looked up and saw the
time. Three o'clock. He remembered immediately one
very important duty. Money must be changed before the
bureaux closed. He had noticed one or two near the
Bourse as the bus had passed early that morning. Now to
these he went. With much politeness, simpering, he
asked the rate of exchange. He spoke in English, for in
money-bureaux with their international customers the
pretence was unnecessary; but he was over-polite, he must

appear at any rate cosmopolitan and no unsmiling insular. He wanted only to *know* the rate, of course; perhaps he would return to-morrow. And so with one rate of exchange noted, he walked out and up the street to another bureau. All money-changers are crooks, he told himself. But the next bureau gave him exactly the same rate. He thanked them and again walked out. His legs were feeling sore again. He stood indecisive for some seconds—then, gritting his teeth, limped round the corner to where a third bureau announced itself. Here, in a negative way, he received more satisfying news. They quoted him a rate lower than the others.

He struggled back to the previous office and there changed a small cheque, enough to keep him going till the next day. The rest he retained—perhaps these three bureaux were in league? There might be others. To-morrow might bring a higher rate. And what about the banks, open in the morning? Or something. Or anything to squeeze out an extra shilling. But at least he was proof against the black market in the streets. He knew about *that*. He knew *all* about the fine rates quoted—and then bad money handed out. There was much bad money about that year. Streets, shops, restaurants were full of people holding money up to the light, like women inspecting the quality of fine silks, to see the watermark. The notes themselves were almost as big as silk handkerchiefs.

He stuffed what had been given him into his trousers pocket. Already it was half-past three. There was not much time left to look for an hotel. It must be decided without much further search. However, with such a chafing between his legs it was plainly impossible to walk. He would operate the second phase of his system. This was to travel quite large distances by bus or tram. On the

way one could see much. He approached the kerb. A
carrozza, an old broken-down affair, flicked its whip at
him and announced itself: 'Carrozza!' The coachman
shouted the word in a way peculiar to the Italian selling
his wares in the street. No question-mark of enquiry, he
simply affirmed it: as though, you felt, one did not know.
Jason smiled and waved it away—he was not going in one
of those, not likely. And along came a tram.

He stepped off the kerb and was just mixing with the
small crowd jostling to enter it when, clicking his tongue
at himself for a fool, he stepped back. He was forgetting
himself! There was something of the greatest importance
left undone! He backed against the wall and, taking out
the roll of money given him by the cashier, did openly
before all eyes what most people—had they done it at all
—would have taken pains to make private. But Jason felt
proud, it was a cleverness that might be advertised; and
any who saw it might well take warning. Separating the
money into different denominations, he selected a tapering five-thousand lire note and folded it into a small packet
—which he wedged then deep into a ticket pocket in
his trousers, by the braces button and over a surface of
the stomach well equipped with nerves. The rest of the
money, the large thousand-lire notes and the thinner
stuff, he divided into three portions. One of these he
placed in the left hip-pocket, the other in the right hip-
pocket—both of which he buttoned securely. The third
portion, a matter of some hundreds, he thrust deeply
down into his trousers pocket, also towards a sensitive
part. He patted each pocket once to feel the little packets
of money in position, straightened his chest, and walked
out to greet the next tram. It had been a gratifying few
seconds, as exquisite as buying a padlock. Also he never
ceased to feel a mixed sense of importance, wealth and

romance at the touch of foreign money. The Italian notes were huge and thick, ugly and as tattered as a currency could be—patched with anyone's length of gummed paper, soiled and crumpled. But however unpleasing such textures may have been, another quality prevailed—the saving grace that it must be spent. Carefully perhaps—but it was a fluid hoarding, in the end gloriously it had to go. And the connotations of its various value were not marked with thrift and graded with the guilts of uneasy profligacy as was the money at home, money doled out by the father, the employer and eventually—never quite unanxious at the parting—by oneself. Alien money is like tipsy money: it parts easily and without regret; the papery umbilical consumes itself with reckless joy.

Jason struggled with the pressing crowd to board that tram. Hot bodies of all kinds surged hard against him; it was difficult with English reticence to manage the rough delicacy of these people. Nobody in fact fought, no touch, however intimate, was personal. Jason was carried up by the scrum. It was all finally needless, because always everybody got on, there were never any left behind: it was only a symptom of native vigour, of an eagerness for action. Once aboard they stood pressed in a firm sausage-like mass along the corridor; somehow the tickets were sold; shins were barked and feet kicked, but nobody complained. And the tram, heavy as a train, clanged at speed up the broad Corso. Wedged, wet with sweat, grubby with touch, Jason stooped awkwardly to see what was passing. He saw no hotel. They came to the station, a broad untidy square sided by the usual heavy barracks of steam. People behind thumped and pushed their way through—it was necessary to worm through the length of the sausage to reach the door for descending. Jason let himself be carried. And was out on the pavement.

Hiding things presupposes their loss. Anxiously his hands went to those four pockets, feeling the little lumps. But they were safe. He boarded another tram, without considering his direction, and industriously, for the next half-hour or more, travelled uncomfortably about the great city. He saw the Capuan gate once, and once the entrance to a great dock; little else of isolated value. By chance one tram took him along the coast-park to Mergellina: he was astounded—an entirely new aspect of Naples presented itself; here on one side stood houses more solid, and on the other, through endless palm gardens, one could see the curve of the sea. One had entered, it seemed, a new bay. Cleaner, more air, and there was the sea—one was orientated towards Vesuvius lying away mistily, one saw to the north quite close the Posillipan cape. The palms looked fresh, the sunny air felt lazed and wealthy, there was a luxus of afternoon in which the serene beautiful place basked its summer. Nor was the tram crowded. But though this, obviously the riviera of residence, appealed—it was for Jason too far from the centre. How could one carry on a proper investigation from such a distance? He returned to the noisier streets that smelled of dust and bad fruit, people and life-soaked walls. A crowded tram, itching with little fingers at his four pockets, took him along the Via Roma. Once, people edged a little away; he had room to search! His hands jumped their fingers out wide and rigid like the legs of a crouched spider. They leapt for his pockets and clutched, each finger tensed directly at its little hidden packet. It looked like a man clutching at pain, at thrusts of lumbago. But the pain passed. The packets were safe.

Weary, he left the tram by the post office. He looked for a café, a bar. Several he paused at, but always forced himself on—what else might lie round the corner, what

treasures, what nostalgia? What gilded whorls announcing a hurdy-gurdy world of SCIROPPI and CIOCCOLATO,
BOMBONI and COLONIALI? What Sicilian travesties of
green and pink and the strange bright turquoise of the
coast? However, once round the post office—which was
something to go round, the Neapolitan Post Office boasted
with reason to be the largest among all the gigantic
Italian post offices, an enormous building of polished
black and grey marble the size of a whole block of buildings—once round, his chafing had become too painful to
go farther, his feet ached like flat feet, and he sat down
opposite the post office in a little modern café with bright
red chairs. There, with his small coffee, he regarded the
monstrous hub of communications and grew morose.
Everything suddenly looked dull. The street revealed
itself as a street. He could see nothing strange in it. Why,
he asked himself, do I travel? Why come all this way?

Why do I imagine I'm living? What do all those people
returning mean when they screw their faces into false
ecstasies and chant: "But that's the *life*, they know how
to *live*." Down South, eh? And what is this gold of Latin
living but an extra dross of selfishness, a grasping-all-
you-can-get openly with none of the reticence of conscience, genuflection to the brother's share? And when I
come all this way, expecting some divine catharsis, some
butterfly ascent from my crabbed old chrysalis—what do
I bring but my dear old self, heaved over the oceans and
the rails, the same dreary old phœnix tottering up from
its immolation of passport and tickets, its ash of caporal
and nazionale? Broaden the mind, see what the other
half does! And is life not confusing enough at home,
without setting oneself a hundred other problems? Does
one see for a moment one's native problems clearer by
observing similar motives in different dress? And while

great thinkers have always taught us that human nature across the world is universally the same (so stay at home, son, with your wife and slippers)—other great thinkers butt in to assert that curiosity is the prime motor of man, that by his nature man must move, man must enquire (so get going, son, put on your boots, get pecking). It is plain that son must stay at home and roam abroad, all at one time, all at the one good time of his sixty years and last ten. Everything is dual: schizophrenia is no sickness, but the natural condition of man, man's motive was always split: like the deepest split of all, the necessity for action and non-action at the same time. We must play both parts, and more, play them with interest. Jason found himself laughing out loud at the post office.

Enough. What about your system? Cleverness A— always travel alone, for otherwise as soon as you might see something of interest, your companion will be sure to point out something else: thus nothing can be digested. Cleverness B—when you're bored abroad, when the onus of loneliness becomes too heavy, when you're fed up with not speaking, and you know that if you do then difficulties of language will make the talk simple and witless—there waits for you Panacea C. Not sleep, not drink nor drug— but the cinema. Go to a film. Any film. Go where it's dark, it's restful, it's insolitary, it's performed technically on your eyes and into your brain—preferably in monochrome. Enjoy the exquisite dream condition, as dreams are usually monochrome. In the cinema you can't move— no interval, no bars, no see-and-be-seen—and there in the half-light you are for three hours rested, pleasantly gregarious, silent. Later you emerge again on to the same southern streets. But with a difference—you have been away; you are reborn; you are there, not for the same first time, but for the second time and all again is new.

Accordingly Jason went to the cinema. Everything turned out as planned—though the seats were hard, and the soundtrack Italian. However—refreshing. And among the films shown was a short document on Naples. What shimmerings, what a having-down in black-and-white! Churches never seen, museums crushed between the restaurants of life, white steamers to Sorrento whose loudspeakers sang "Farewell, Sorrento." (To-morrow Jason would go to such churches, smelling their waxen candle smoke, peering at musty dolls and dusty paper— nothing would be clear, nothing black-and-white.) And the cool museums, tormentors of feet, blurrers of the eyes! Flitting easily from one place to another, with no tired feet, the camera took him to the Garden of Oranges, to the Villa Floridana, to the Cathedral, to a monastery and to the bathing beaches. Up and down funiculars, out to the grim old Castel dell'Ovo—a glittering black corrugation against a silver sea—past palms set against the sky and gay-harnessed mules photographed clean and clear against bright sunlit white walls. Where the ubiquitous smearing and dust? Where was the smell? This clear-cut city of black-and-white had nothing in common with the golden-hazed, pullulating heap of merged surfaces, of sunbaked plaster and mouldering stone, that constituted the real city of his day.

Nevertheless, he left the cinema considerably refreshed. Emerging on to the street, the city greeted him anew; everything looked fresh and interesting. But it was already late in the afternoon—it was vital to fix an hotel. He decided to abandon his search for the terraced ideal— obviously such hotels did not exist—and turned determined into the first hotel he saw. It was full. And so was the second, and so the third. His superiority trembled away, it was necessary now to beg for a room, and any

room. He found himself bowing and simpering to the
blue-jowled, self-assured men who sat so negligently at
their reception desks. At last, after a most disagreeable
half-hour, he was accommodated in a barely furnished
barracks for commercial travellers.

It was seven stories high: he was on the sixth. There
was no lift. Underneath, the trams groaned and clattered
ceaselessly. But—though there were neither courtyards
nor fountains nor vine-clad verandahs—it was cheap;
and however high one climbed in Naples, one found oneself always on another plane of life—balconies opposite
and around him composed a busy new platform of existence. Here again was a solid street life of pots and pans
and tubs of flowers, music and washing; and the lowering
of buckets on long ropes to the street accentuated this
feeling of a separate ground-level in the sky.

After he had fetched his luggage and informed the
receptionist that he might only be staying one night—
reviving thus his treasured independence, letting himself
in for nothing—he washed and lay on the bed, considering what next could be done. Six o'clock. He had discovered where the centre of the Piedigrotta festival took
place. The main thing was to avoid Dale and that other
man Hislop.

Seven o'clock found him edging near Zi' Teresa.
Already he was primed with grappa, drunk disconsolately
in several small bars, already he was tired of his own company. It was difficult to contrive an Italian bar acquaintance. Such as he spoke to either regarded him as some
sort of luscious prey, or proved most amiable, kind and
pleasant—but soon went off into their own infernal language, leaving him uselessly silent and uncomprehending.
The minutes, the half-hours ticked away! At five past
seven he was shaking hands with Dale and Hislop, ex-

changing wonderful greetings in English, sitting down to
drinks, delighted.

And with the drinks—long-stemmed glasses of sooth-
ing gold spumanti, clear and fresh, needling the dry
tongue with ice-cold bubbles, tasting sweetly of the grape
itself—Jason grew tolerant and comfortable. Without
noticing it, he talked as much as Dale. Dale's informative
discourse began to sound brilliant, of deep interest. The
sun sank and turned the sea from gold to embered rose,
then to bright fire streaked with pale translucent olive.
Violet shadows deepened behind Vesuvius. Over all the
vast bay the sky grew tumultuous with colour—such
colour that is said sometimes to be vulgar, cheap, and of
the chocolate box by artists over-clever and jaded—and
soon a chain of lights began to twinkle all round the coast
as in turn, with a sudden sinking swiftness, those colours
faded and sky, sea and land deepened to indigo.

Dale, keen Dale, talk on! Talk, as the white table-cloth
assumes its night lustre, as the white-coated waiters dance
to and fro, as the smooth and black waters of the little
port reflect long bars of gold in their lapping darkness; as
out on the broader bay a battle-ship's lights proclaim a
ballroom in the sea; as oarsmen lean forward on their oars
and slide their boats from darkness to light and again into
darkness; as the wine is sipped, as the night air blows
warm, as music of the mandolin rings its shrill opera from
the quay. Talk, Dale—tell us of this ancient place, tell us
of Micenus the trumpeter whose cape we see ahead,
stretch your hand to indicate Circe, talk of the dead who
still impress themselves on the multitudes of to-day. And
look!—away up across the sky fires the first artifice, the
priapic golden rocket bursting high against the night
with balls of emerald and bright ruby, fishing lights
tossed and lost in the ancient heaven. Another, another—

and each flaring our faces with weird carnival light, each
stamping the night with sudden glorious thunder! Dale—
they're shooting things up into the sky, they're obeying
their ancient premises, they're carving towers of fire and
spurting up their plenty to the gods!

And Hislop, more practical Hislop—no word from
you? None but a lulled, sun-tanned smile, confident of the
evening? But perhaps as well—let us instead all join
together and imbibe this ancient place and this later land
of opera. Where uniforms can be green, where a green
and red and white flag sails over a yellow-and-green land,
where the cockaded carabinieri may sport the old Bour-
bonish scarlet-trimmed blue—but cannot help but stand
against yellow walls, or against the thick green of plants
that splay copiously without order and never stand in
lines like the trees of other lands. This earth so full of
song, this arid south so virile! . . . There! There flies
another sweet eruption, its fiery trail sparking like the
bubbles at my throat! . . .

So, warming, they dined; dined well at old Teresa's on
the waterfront, among the middle-class plump herd, a
jostling laughing lot like faces from the previous century.
No more trouble now in Jason's clever heart, the heart
grew warm, and no tragedies overcame his less anxious
plate—bulbous pink prawns in a bed of rice, partridge,
zabaglione. Gradually, as these good things and more
wine went down, the aperture of his eyes seemed to close,
or grow intimate and close—no longer could one half-see
all round one, but one looked straight and with keen
pleasure at the nearest tables, the nearest face, positions
and laughter . . . one made warm pictures, the background
faded. Fireworks played intermittently—for this was only
a warming up, a spangling before the grand cannonade to
be loosed later. At nine o'clock they rose and strolled up

the quay and along under the palms of the promenade gardens. A great moon, heavy and golden, rose like a lantern over Sorrento.

They strolled in the gardens, and then into the streets. More illuminations received them there—whole artificial churches of electric bulbs spanned the streets, lines and curves of bulbing like pearls extended the length of the tramlined road to Mergellina. Flags and streamers festooned the windows, music sounded from great canopied roundabouts and flying swings, on one balcony a lifesize paper gondola swung its Chinese lantern slowly to and fro. The taverns were full, all Naples had turned out into these streets. And everywhere street-sellers sold soft balls with elastic strings, balls that were thrown everywhere at anyone, rebounding with laughter back to the hand. Twice, though, Jason felt a wave of sadness—one does not change absolutely with a little wine. He reflected that whereas he could never walk the daylit streets without attracting more sharks and touts than other people (did he look so simple?), nevertheless he could walk through a carnival crowd and remain it seemed the only one unaccosted with a laughing ball, a streamer (did he look so cold, so unlovable?). And once he felt a twinge of the old superiority when he saw several carrozzas full of white-clad sailors off the American battleship—fools, he thought, you'll be caught in a way I won't. The carrozzas wheeled by, the inelegant sailors sprawled but happy, singing and smoking cigars that looked bawdy sticking from such trim sea-washed faces. The drivers flicked their whips, the cavalcade was gone; but a little whip flicked in Jason's heart—had he perhaps been watching the sailors with regret? Then they turned into one of those dark caverns and brightened themselves with a carafe of red wine. He felt again better.

By the time the pyrotechnic crisis occurred he was elated beyond recovery. The Italian came now fluently from his mouth—languages are faith, not application—and he was smiling easily at all around him. At last a girl had thrown a ball at his ear. And then suddenly, as they walked towards the sea, a tremendous sound like the eruption of an arsenal filled the bay with gunfire and ominous rumbling echoes.

So many at once—there was the beauty . . . not for the Neapolitan your slow motion of set-pieces, your pretty patterns and your economy of rocket. No, all must go up at once. Homage to Vesuvius, homage to the old monster . . . thus from a hundred boats, from all the set ambuscades there rose at one time a dreadful arrowing of fire, flashing wide orange light over the indigo bay, outblazing the moon and soaring high up to burst together in a shower of savage colour—a detonation that left a godlike pall of smoke high and huge, a sullen canvas against which now broke more and ever more shapes of fire, liquid fire like bright paint splashing over the glowing canvas, emerald and ruby and gold stars glittering with the wicked brilliance of tinsel . . . all to a thunder of sound, ever-growing, cracking and redoubling viciously as the crescendo of colour grew and spread ever more thickly over the sky . . . more and more . . . faster and faster . . . stealing the breath, aweing, frightening—as though indeed something were out of control, something savage as a forest fire . . . roaring ever greater . . . until as many as had burst before all went up together in one vast convulsive hymn, one ultimate chord to the iridescent dazzling sky. . . .

Like a curtain the night dropped; a last misdirected squiblike thing petered away to one side; then the moon appeared ghostly through the quiet, very distant cloud of smoke. A great sigh went up from the crowd.

That breath, exalted and dedicated, from the thousand dark figures murmuring against the moon's light—that sigh of human-hearted wonder echoed itself on in Jason's breast. He swelled with admiration, with pride—as though he himself had contrived these marvels. And it was exactly midnight!—this completed the day . . . and just then he felt that he had won Naples, he had 'got' the city. The day might have seen reverses—but the very fact that he had struggled on, never giving in, proved an essay of faith that was in itself the stuff of achievement. But now this climactic evening was not itself ended—the crowd now turned back from the sea to the streets—these streets he knew stretched right round the long promenade, far round the bay; and as a festive crowd will, it gave out over a great distance an effusion of small subtle sound, almost inaudible, like the murmuring of a metropolis heard from a suburb. Such sound kept the streets open, it gave no sense of the night ever finishing, people would be surging round every corner, there would be no dead patches—lights on, doors open, tables crammed! Good Dale, faithful Hislop—come . . . he took their arms and again they were off past the naphtha flares, the gaslit faces, the palms, into the electric-bulbed bubbling streets. Exalted he sang out:

"See Naples—and die!"

Dale swung round at him, not glittering, but now peering muzzily with his spectacles:

"Vide Neapolis et——"

"Virgil wrote them here, here, exactly *here*!"

Jason stamped on the cobbled gutter, stopping the other two, swaying slightly. Dale said, mock-haughtily:

"The Georgics were indeed written here; but at the present I refer to something quite else—to a message, misquoted for ever after—'Vide Napoli et—et . . .' anyway, 'Vide,' it said, 'See Naples and afterwards a town called—called . . .' anyway, a town along the coast that sounds like the Latin for death—and ever since——"

Jason's heart flowed with goodwill. Dale, good tolerant Dale, Dale making mistakes, Dale with his armour pierced, now laughing. . . . Then suddenly, seeing a restaurant opposite, he cried:

"Pizzi—come on, on me——"

But as he said it, his hand clutched his pocket, he was rocked, he was thrown off his balance because he had no more money, or at least not enough even for those pancakes, the last five hundred lire he had watched go an hour ago . . . and where were the little packets? Hidden. Hidden in the bedroom before he had left. One underneath the wash-basin, one in a shoe, one in a locked drawer. He had brought out only enough for a night's amusement. Suddenly his hand hit on something hard, the buttoned hip-pocket of these fresh trousers he had put on for the evening, and this hard thing was his wallet, his beloved wallet left buttoned-up in the locked case and now carelessly worn throughout the evening! A clap of guilt flushed him as he realized his dreadful mistake, his risk. Inside the wallet he knew rested his pink return ticket to the frontier, and his green return ticket home from there to Paris and across the dangerous Channel to safe Kent, Kent of the tea-urns and the green railway-coaches, Kent of the sick-tired travellers and the reliable porters! He shuddered as he saw how nearly he might have lost it—for none of Jason's journeys was complete, none unanxious until that last green return ticket was safely torn. Then, as he shuddered, he felt notes—five pound sterling notes! New-minted, fresh—a safety-cache, but now to-night imminently spendable. He looked round. But that slight whispering always a foot away for once was absent. It had been there all day. But now the few yards round them were empty, nobody stood near.

He realized that they had collected no touts because the group of them for once looked active and interested in themselves. So shouting to the others to wait, he moved off and stood alone looking at a barrow. Simultaneously another sense told him that this was precisely what all day he had been avoiding; and another warned him that he would appear intoxicated enough to invite a 'doing,' even if the tout might be honest; and another said that he was really drunk enough to be done by anyone faster than ever before; and yet another told him that he was great and cute enough to see through anyone; and another that the evening and he were charmed and thus that nothing bad could befall. He continued to stand there.

Not more than a minute later a voice was strolling up to him:

"Changez argent?"

No whispering—perhaps because this was night, and night condones the dark trades—and the wizened face of the boy who looked up at him winked whitely and smiled, as though between Jason and him there was some known conspiracy. To this Jason warmed, as also he was flattered to be taken for a Frenchman. He smiled and nodded, explaining that he might have some pounds sterling. And that quick boy changed instantly into English, brightening his lined face as though a meeting with Jason was the greatest good fortune that could happen to him. It was.

They were standing in the light of a flare on a barrow selling fruit, flowers and sweets. Dyed plants like feathers, magenta and vicious lemon, sprayed up against a sheath of turquoise paper; crimson water-melons dribbled their black pips; nougats and green almond pastes glittered in tissue and tinfoil; hot scarlet flowers glowed palely in the fierce naphtha light—palely as cigarette-tips in the sun. In this light the boy stood, the young man of twenty, already old in face and thin-haired, his ragged coat and wide trousers fitting him like the odd suit of a clown. Beneath the smile hung an urgency—the forces of argument gathering? But this might have been no more than the inner energy that hides behind all Italian eyes, the light of passions consuming always within. So that Jason paid little attention—such a light will shine at all times, while simply waiting for a train, or bathing in the sun—and asked the boy what price he could give. Then began an elaborate business.

The boy waved to a man standing in the half-light some yards off. The man beckoned to the boy, the boy asked Jason if he would step over to his friend, who 'knew prices.' Jason went, but moving out of the naphtha light he felt suddenly on guard; not in danger, rather alert and amused, for the wine still held him in its confidence. The two others talked fast in Italian. Suddenly the boy broke off, turned round and suggested a price. Jason immediately shook his head, requiring more. Another swift interchange in Italian, and then the boy turned and said:

"This price is difficult. But we will try arrange it— you come with my friend and we see another friend, negociant, understand?"

"Come on, better come away. Don't trust this street-stuff."

It was Dale's voice suddenly from behind his shoulder. But Jason knew his strength:

"That's all right, I won't be a moment. You go back and order the pizzi."

"I think we'll come too."

"Nonsense. I can tackle this."

"Might as well stroll along, nothing to do, see some life——"

It crossed Jason's mind that if they were going up one of the narrow sidestreets, then three would certainly be better company than one. So he laughed, agreed, started off after the two men—though he still determined to handle things himself. However, they went up no sidestreet, simply along the main road to where streamers and a bright neon light advertised a bar. The two boys in front moved fast, hurrying; in the bar they found the man they sought, leaning with a coffee. The matter was discussed again. Jason was about to suggest a drink when the first boy came over:

"He says yes, he can give the price. You come out with us, too much people here."

Together then the six of them left, it seemed as if in a mob, as if excited by a matter far more urgent than such a small money deal. This time they turned off down a sidestreet. The boy, winking up at Jason:

"No policemans."

Having now drunk no wine for some time, Dale and Hislop had become quieter; but Jason was excited still, drunk on the tide of initiative. The three Neapolitans walked in front, leading the way; they were of one size, short and light, more boys than men it seemed, and they all moved nimbly, accustomed to those pavements. They hardly looked dangerous—though the street itself grew shabbier and less comforting.

Suddenly they stopped, edged into a doorway slightly lit by a street-lamp, and signed back to Jason. The boy said:

"Here we can change. You got the pounds?"

Jason drew out his pocket-book, all heads came to-

shone down at the far end. They ran straight at this light. They were silhouetted plainly and they ran in the middle of the street. None of them looked back, they ran straight ahead like boys, knees doubled up high and small tight fists battled at their chests—like small boys on the sand, their stomachs pulling them along, their legs galloping before them. No great strides, no outflung arms, no lancing forward at the shadows—this was a tight, ruthless, efficient locomotion, they were machines with everything decided before, the three acting as one. Perhaps that they were three was most startling of all. They disappeared round the corner, gone; and those other three felt that they had seen something classic, the fearful escapade of ragamuffins.

Jason looked down at the bundle of lire in his hand. With surprise he saw it was still there!

"W—ell!" He let out that long breath that had been for seconds held. In the half-light he looked round at the others' shadowy faces and made a look of surprise.

Hislop muttered:

"You've been done, the bastards!"

wards it. He held it very firmly and showed the five one-pound notes. A hand came out towards them. But he drew back, smiling politely to offset the gesture:

"Where are the lire?"

The boy smiled his wizened smile, and produced from inside that ragged coat a large bundle of lira notes. Jason said:

"You don't mind if I look at them, do you? There's so much bad money about—business matter, no offence?"

Dale and Hislop stood silent to either side of them. All six men's eyes watched carefully, though their six mouths smiled. The boy handed Jason one of the lire notes. Jason held it up to the light, noted the watermark, ran his finger over it to see there was no wax impression. The note was good. The boy was smiling and nodding:

"Good, eh? All good here."

It was not often that Jason had the courage to insist on checking money or bills in front of people—as with the waiters. But in his present mood, with time to spare and with the others at his elbow, he was determined that this deal should be watertight. Thus he took—exactly as he should have done—every precaution. His mind worked keenly, he made no mistake. At first the boy did not want him to count all the notes, but he insisted. Very carefully

But Jason knew. He laughed easily:

"Nonsense, the stuff's here all right, counted, checked. They probably thought I might change my mind—or wanted to get off quickly from the scene of crime."

"Bet they slipped you one. Look."

Jason did. As he unfolded the bundle he saw with alarm that the outer note was not as before a note of five hundred lire, but now of a hundred denomination—coloured roughly the same. And inside this first sheaf was a bundle of white shaving paper.

"They scarcely use it for anything else," hissed Dale.